It was a show about missing people, and it had an eight-hundred number that it ran on the bottom of the screen all show long. If you stared at the number too long, it kind of hypnotized you. I made my eyes go in and out of focus, and after about ten minutes I was feeling a little high, so I kept the show on.

"We now have a story that's all too typical of American life today," the narrator said. He was one of those actors who used to be on lots of TV series. Dad would have recognized him. I was feeling too eight-hundredy to try. "This is a story about the most common type of childhood abduction in America, when a noncustodial parent steals a little child from her rightful home."

I may only be sixteen, but one thing I know is there are moments in your life when all you have to do is change the channel and everything comes out completely different. I didn't change the channel.

ALSO AVAILABLE IN LAUREL-LEAF BOOKS:

TWICE
TAKEN

SUSAN BETH PFEFFER

LAUREL-LEAF BOOKS

Published by
Bantam Doubleday Dell Books for Young Readers
a division of
Bantam Doubleday Dell Publishing Group, Inc.
1540 Broadway
New York, New York 10036

The trademark Laurel-Leaf Library® is registered in the
U.S. Patent and Trademark Office.
The trademark Dell® is registered in the U.S. Patent and
Trademark Office.

ISBN: 0-440-22004-1

RL: 4.7

Reprinted by arrangement with Delacorte Press

Printed in the United States of America

June 1996

10 9 8 7 6 5 4 3 2

OPM

1

I never would have called the eight-hundred number if I hadn't been so angry at Dad.

I was mad at him because he'd made a date with Charleen (who I didn't much like), and when Charleen's baby-sitter chickened out, I was told I'd have to stay with her kids (who I really hated). It was a Saturday night, and I had plans to go out with a bunch of kids I knew to movies and pizza. No official dates, but Jason Best was also going, and I was kind of hot for him. But Dad and Charleen came first, at least as far as Dad was concerned.

I guess I'd let him know just what I thought about all this in the car when he drove us to Charleen's, but he chose to misinterpret my feelings, which only made me angrier. "Don't worry, honey," he said to me. "I'll never get serious about Charleen. Not with those monsters of hers."

In other words I was losing a chance at Jason Best so Dad could go out with a woman he wasn't even going to be serious about. By the time we got to Charleen's, my face had frozen into a permanent scowl.

"This is so nice of you, Brooke," Charleen said to me as Dad and I walked in. "I have so few chances to go out and have fun. You have no idea what it's like being a single mother."

"It's no picnic being a single father either," Dad said, which really made me homicidal.

"Now, kids, I'm going out with Paul," Charleen said. "And I won't be getting back until way after your bedtimes. I want you to brush your teeth and say your prayers and be nice to Brooke. All right?"

"Don't go, Mommy," little monster Tiffany cried. "I hate Paul!"

Paul hates you too, kid, I thought, but I didn't say it.

"Now, don't be silly, Tiffany sweetie," Charleen said. "You'll have a wonderful time here with Brooke. Give Mommy a kiss. You too, Brian."

"I'm too old to kiss," Brian said, edging into a corner.

"Don't go, Mommy!" Tiffany shrieked. "Please!"

Charleen did the sensible thing. She grabbed her pocketbook and my father, and left me to deal with the mess.

Tiffany kept screaming for a while, until Brian threw his baseball glove at her. Then she screamed even louder.

"Brian," I said. I wouldn't have minded the technique if it had worked.

"He hit me!" Tiffany shouted. She ran over to me and kicked me in the leg, I suppose to get my attention.

"Don't kick," I said, looking down at what was going

2

to be a gigantic black-and-blue mark. No skirts for me for the next few days.

"I hate you!" Tiffany shouted, maybe to me, maybe to Brian. Brian thought that was funny and threw a teddy bear at Tiffany. I started to regard everything in Charleen's living room as a potential weapon.

"How about something to eat?" I asked. "Maybe your mother left some cookies or something."

"I want Mommy!" Tiffany yelled. She kicked me again for emphasis.

"Listen, you stupid idiot, kicking me isn't going to bring your mommy back," I said. "So stop it already."

Tiffany, ever cynical, kicked me a third time. Brian started laughing. He laughed so hard that the *TV Guide* he threw at his sister hit me instead.

"No more throwing!" I yelled.

Tiffany meanwhile had grabbed hold of my waist and was giving me short, powerful jabs with her right foot. Brian had mercifully vanished into the kitchen. I tried to pull Tiffany away from me, when I saw Brian returning with a carton of eggs. He took one of the eggs out and was just about to throw it when I shook myself free of Tiffany, who landed on her fanny. That really made her scream.

"NO THROWING!" I screamed. "Brian, if you even think about throwing that egg, I will personally kill you."

Who could resist an offer like that? Certainly not Brian, who gave the egg a healthy toss in my direction. I ducked, and the egg splatted on an end table.

Tiffany thought that was a riot. She stopped crying long enough to join Brian and start tossing eggs at me too.

Do you blame me for being angry at Dad?

Two of the eggs actually hit me, although neither did any real damage. Not to me, at any rate, but Charleen's living room was starting to look like an omelet factory.

There was no point trying to stop them, and fortunately the box wasn't full. Once they'd thrown the last egg, Brian and Tiffany were both in much better spirits.

"You promised us cookies," Brian said.

"I want cookies," Tiffany said.

"Eat all the cookies you want," I told them. It was my most solemn hope that they'd eat so many, they'd throw up in their sleep and choke on their own vomit.

Brian ran to the kitchen for the cookie raid, and Tiffany ran after him, only she slipped on an egg yoke and fell. That got her crying again. It didn't help her mood any that Brian and I both started laughing.

"I want my mommy!" Tiffany howled.

The problem was my father wanted her too, and when Dad wanted a woman, he tended to go after her. Not that there'd been an endless string. But ever since he and Mona divorced, and that was over three years ago, he'd spent most of his Saturday nights out. Which was fine with me, as long as I had the same privilege.

"Mommy, Mommy," Tiffany was crying. Brian had brought the bag of cookies into the living room and was eating them right next to her. She looked up at him, whimpered, and Brian reached down to help her up. Only, once she was supporting herself on him, he slipped his hand away, and down went Tiffany all over again.

"That does it!" I said. "Brian, into your bedroom. Tiffany, into yours."

"I didn't do anything," Brian said. "She tripped."

"I want my mommy!" Tiffany said.

"Out!" I yelled. They didn't move.

"I have an idea," I said, like they would care. "Why don't you go into your mother's bedroom and watch a movie." I took a quick look at the videotape library. "How about *Bambi*?" I asked. "Or *Fantasia*?"

"*Terminator*!" Brian yelled. He ran to the tapes and pulled it out.

"*Terminator*!" Tiffany said, following her big brother into their mother's room. I listened as they turned the TV on, put the tape in, and started yelling contentedly with the action. I closed the door, went back to the living room, and cursed my father for several minutes. Then I looked around for something to do.

There really wasn't anything. Charleen didn't believe in books, or if she did, she kept them hidden. The living room consisted of furniture, lots of toys, and some smashed eggs, which I wasn't about to clean up. I remembered then that neither Dad nor Charleen had mentioned my getting paid for the baby-sitting, and I realized they probably had no intention of paying me. I was family, after all, and family helps out for free. I only wished there were some more eggs left.

I couldn't spend the evening talking on the phone, because all my friends were out, including Jason Best. That only left TV, and even that wasn't so great. The good TV, the one with cable and the VCR, was in Charleen's bedroom. The network-only TV was in the living room with me. I was so desperate at that point, I turned it on. Only little kids and old people watched network TV on a Saturday night. But it was better than sitting and staring at egg yolks.

All I did was channel-flip, which was hard since there wasn't any remote, and I had to sit by the TV and do it myself. I went around the stations (and there were only six of them) three times, looking for anything not too horribly boring.

I ended up on Channel 6, mostly because the reception was better than on any of the other stations. They were showing something I'd never seen before, a series called *Still Missing*. I wasn't surprised I'd never seen it. I don't usually spend my Saturday nights watching TV.

It was a show about missing people, and it had an eight-hundred number that it ran on the bottom of the screen all show long. If you stared at the number too long, it kind of hypnotized you. I made my eyes go in and out of focus, and after about ten minutes I was feeling a little high, so I kept the show on.

"We now have a story that's all too typical of American life today," the narrator said. He was one of those actors who used to be on lots of TV series. Dad would have recognized him. I was feeling too eight-hundredy to try. "This is a story about the most common type of childhood abduction in America, when a noncustodial parent steals a little child from her rightful home."

I may only be sixteen, but one thing I know is there are moments in your life when all you have to do is change the channel and everything comes out completely different. I didn't change the channel.

"This is Betty Girard," the narrator said. They showed her then too, a pleasant-looking woman, standing with her pleasant-looking husband and their two pleasant-looking children. "Eleven years ago, Betty Girard's daughter, Amy, was kidnapped, presumably by Amy's father."

I kept watching. I even let my eyes get focused again.

"Betty last saw Amy when Amy was only five years old," the narrator said. I suddenly remembered his name. Lloyd Carson. He was on a cop show Dad used to watch. "Amy's father took her for his once-a-month weekend visit, but he never brought Amy back home. Tell us, Betty, what happened next."

"I called his home, and there was no answer," Betty said. "Mike, my husband, drove over to Hal's place. Hal is my ex, Amy's father. He lived about a hundred miles away, and by the time Mike got there, there was no sign of Hal or Amy."

"The super let me in," Mike Girard said. "The apartment was completely empty. It was as though nobody had ever lived there."

"I called the police to report Amy missing," Mrs. Girard said. "But they weren't very helpful. They said there was probably a mix-up in the plans. I begged them to start looking for Amy, but they said they had no jurisdiction over custody disputes and I should just wait it out."

"The laws have changed since that fateful day," Lloyd Carson declared. "Nowadays the police take a report like Betty's very seriously. But it took a lot of pain and suffering before they changed, and some of that suffering belongs to the Girard family. Tell us, Betty, what you did next."

"I was terrified," Betty said. "I knew, I just knew, Hal had stolen my child. I even called his mother, but she said she hadn't heard from him, and I believed her. Hal had very little contact with his family. I didn't know any of his friends, so we waited until the next morning and called the place where he worked. They said he'd handed in his notice on Friday."

"So this had all been planned," Lloyd Carson said. "The kidnapping of your little girl, Amy."

"We hired a private investigator," Mike Girard said. "Believe me, it wasn't easy on a schoolteacher's salary to find the money for one, but we did. There were a couple of leads he thought were promising, but he never found Amy."

"We registered her with all the missing-children's organizations," Mrs. Girard said. "Her picture was printed on shopping bags and milk cartons."

"And the years went on," Lloyd Carson said. "And life went on."

"Three years after Amy disappeared, we had Timmy," Mrs. Girard said, hugging an eight-year-old boy. He didn't seem real eager to be hugged on national TV, but at least he wasn't throwing eggs at anybody. "We love Holly and Timmy with all our hearts, but there's a piece of our family that's missing, and that's Amy."

"Amy was a bright little five-year-old," Lloyd Carson declared. I guessed someone had told him that, because otherwise I didn't see how he could know. "She knew her alphabet and how to count by the age of four. Although she had not yet started kindergarten at the time of her abduction, she was already reading." They showed a couple of pictures of Amy. She was cute, but then again so was Tiffany when she wasn't kicking and screaming.

"In many ways my life has been wonderful," Mrs. Girard said. "Mike and Holly and Timmy are all pretty perfect."

They showed a videotape of the family while she was talking. They were saying grace at the dinner table, heads bowed down, hands joined together. Then they showed them at Christmas opening all their presents under the tree. They looked like every family you've ever dreamed of. I began to feel sorry for Amy, missing out on all that love.

"The Girards never gave up searching or praying for Amy's return," Lloyd Carson said. "That's why they were so excited when they read about a new technique being used with great success in finding missing children."

"I read about it in a magazine," Mrs. Girard said. "The article said you could take a picture of a very young child and a computer can create an image of what that child would look like five, even ten years later."

"So the Girards took several pictures of Amy to the Mackenzie Computer Enhancement Facility in Maryville, New Jersey," Lloyd Carson said.

"They asked us to bring at least three," Mr. Girard said. "Preferably one full face and two different profile shots."

"We made a special point of taking a picture that showed Amy with her father," Mrs. Girard said. "Even at age five, people commented on how much Amy resembled her father."

"From these eleven-year-old pictures Mackenzie Computer Enhancement Facility specialists were able to figure out a great deal about Amy's current appearance," Lloyd Carson said. "How tall she is, how much she weighs, even her hair color. From this photograph of a five-year-old child, they were able to create this portrait of a sixteen-year-old."

The funny thing was, I didn't recognize myself from the computer-enhanced whatever. It really didn't look all that much like me. And while Mr. and Mrs. Girard looked mildly familiar, there was no moment when I jumped up and yelled "Mommy!" No, the only way I knew they were talking about me was when they flashed the picture of Amy's dad. Him I would have recognized anywhere. I hadn't thought about that mustache in years—Mona persuaded him to shave it off—but that was my dad all right, and that meant I had to be Amy.

They showed the computer picture a few seconds longer, to give all of America who was home on Saturday night watching network TV a chance to recognize her. And the eight-hundred number kept right on rolling on the bottom of the TV screen.

I turned the sound down on the TV. I could hear Brian and Tiffany screaming in Charleen's bedroom. I wasn't sure, but it sounded like Brian was strangling Tiffany. No great loss to humanity.

Mr. and Mrs. Girard and their perfect children were still on the show, so I turned the sound back on. "Please come back, Amy," the little boy was saying. "Amy, we miss you," the girl said, with considerably less conviction.

"Amy will always be my firstborn," Mrs. Girard said. "I will never rest until I find her and bring her back home."

I turned the TV off then, feeling kind of bad for them and all the money they'd spent searching for Amy—for me, if you want to be technical about it—and then I got angry at Dad all over again. Not because he stole me. I knew that he had, and I'd made my peace with that years ago, even though he had told me my mother had made no effort to track me down and that seemed to be a lie. No, I got mad at him because he picked Charleen over me and left me stuck watching network TV on a Saturday night. I didn't know much about Mr. and Mrs. Girard, but at least neither of them was dating Charleen.

So I called the eight-hundred number. I certainly knew it by heart from staring at it for twenty minutes. "*Still Missing* Hot Line," a woman said. "How may we help you?"

"You just showed something about a missing girl," I said. "Amy something. I'm not sure what her last name is."

"The Girard family," the woman said. "Do you have any information about Amy?"

"I think I'm her," I said. "I mean, I'm really pretty sure I'm her."

"Hold on one second," the woman said. "Whatever you do, don't hang up. All right, Amy?"

"Sure," I said. I can't describe how unreal all this felt. Dad and Charleen were out, and given the fact I wasn't home either, they'd go back to the apartment, our apartment, and spend their quality time there. There was still about an hour and a half left on *The Terminator*, and with any luck Tiffany would fall asleep while she was watching it and I'd just carry her to her bedroom. The hell with prayers and brushing teeth. Brian would stay up awhile longer, but he wasn't so bad when you got him alone and unarmed.

Charleen would have to decide where she was spending the night, but I suspected it would be at Dad's, just because the opportunity was there. I'd sack out on the living-room sofa, and the next morning, around six, they'd show up, so Charleen would officially be home before the kids woke up. Dad and I would go back to our place, and I'd sleep until noon. Dad would make pancakes for us, and I'd call Katie and Maria, my two best friends, and find out about the movie and the pizza and Jason. Then homework, and TV, and bed. That's what was going to happen. I knew it as well as I knew my own name.

"Hello, Amy?" a man said. "This is Ralph Torrez, head of the *Still Missing* Hot Line. How are you?"

"I'm fine," I said.

"What makes you so sure you are Amy?" he asked.

"Well, I'm sixteen," I said. "And I live with my dad, and I know my parents are divorced, only I haven't seen my mother in years, I was five or six, I really don't remember just when, and mostly I recognized a picture of my dad." I had my first stab of guilt when I said that.

"You're sure that was a picture of your father," Mr. Torrez said. "There's no chance you were mistaken?"

"I know my father," I said. "That was him."

"Does your father know you're calling?" Mr. Torrez asked.

"No," I said. "He's out on a date."

"Do you expect him back immediately?" Mr. Torrez asked.

"No," I said. "Not for hours."

"Give us your address and phone number," Mr. Torrez said.

"You mean my home address?" I asked. "Or where I am now?"

"Both," Mr. Torrez said. "Start with where you are now."

So I did.

"Why aren't you at home?" he asked.

"I'm baby-sitting," I said. "My dad's date's kids."

"Is there any chance your father and his date will be returning there soon?" Mr. Torrez asked.

"Not a chance," I said.

"Very well," Mr. Torrez said. "Amy, we're going to call the police in your town right now and ask them to go to your current address. If this is a prank, tell us immediately, or else you could be in serious trouble."

"It's no prank," I said, kind of angry. Here I was, getting ready to bring joy to Mr. and Mrs. Girard and their perfect children, and some stranger was asking me if I was playing a prank.

"Very well," Mr. Torrez said. "Stay where you are, and keep talking to us. We're putting in the call to the police right now, and they should be there in minutes. Can you do that, Amy?"

"I guess," I said. I wished he'd stop calling me Amy. My name was Brooke.

"While we're on the phone, why don't you tell me about your father," Mr. Torrez said. "We know him as Hal Donovan. Does he still use that name?"

Donovan. That was the second jab that evening, almost as strong as the one I'd felt seeing Dad's picture on TV. Amy Donovan. Amy Something Donovan. I closed my eyes, and my brain started chanting "A, my name is Amy and my husband's name is Al." Amy Something Donovan.

"Michelle," I said.

"Your father goes by the name Michelle?" Mr. Torrez asked. I don't know what he thought. Maybe Dad had had a sex-change operation.

"No, Michelle was my middle name," I said. "Amy Michelle Donovan."

"You're right," Mr. Torrez said, and I felt an unreasonable surge of pride. I'd showed him I knew who I was. Amy Michelle Donovan, stuck in an egg-soaked apartment with two monsters because she had a father who didn't care enough about his only daughter to change his plans for one stinking evening.

"Amy Michelle Donovan," Mr. Torrez said. "Welcome home."

2

The doorbell rang. I thought, *I won't answer it, and then none of this will have happened.*

"Was that the doorbell?" Mr. Torrez asked. "If it's the police, let me speak to them."

I thought about saying it wasn't the doorbell, but they started knocking then, and one of them said "Police" so loudly, there was no way Mr. Torrez could be fooled. I opened the door, and there were two officers, a man and a woman, standing there. "Amy Donovan?" the woman asked. She smiled at me, I guess to reassure me they weren't about to shoot.

"Mr. Torrez wants to speak to you," I said. "On the phone."

The man went to the phone and said hello. He didn't say much after that, so I figured Mr. Torrez was doing most of the talking. Somehow that didn't surprise me.

"This must be pretty exciting for you," the police-woman said. "Being on national TV and all."

"Exciting, yeah," I said.

The policeman hung up the phone, so I never had a chance to say good-bye to Mr. Torrez. "We're going to take you to the station house," he said.

"Should I get a lawyer?" I asked. It seemed like a sensible enough question, but the two officers laughed.

"You're not under arrest," the policewoman said. "It's just this is a matter for Social Services, and their offices are closed for the evening."

"A caseworker will meet us at the station," the policeman said. "Don't worry, Amy. By tomorrow you should be with your mother."

"That'll be nice," I said. My mother. Now, there was a concept I hadn't been dealing with for quite a while.

"Come on, honey," the policewoman said. "Let's get you out of here before your father shows up."

"Wait a second," I said. "I can't just leave. I'm baby-sitting."

"I'll see if one of the neighbors can look after the kids," the policeman said. "You stay here with Amy, Sal."

"Okay," the policewoman said. The policeman left the apartment and started knocking on people's doors. *It would take a cop to get neighbors to watch Brian and Tiffany*, I thought. It's hard to say no to a gun.

I looked at the policewoman. She seemed nice enough. "Can I make a phone call?" I asked.

"Sure," she said.

The funny thing was, I didn't know who to call. I thought of Dad, but he was still out, and besides, I didn't want to leave a message explaining everything while the policewoman was still around. I didn't know if he was going to be in trouble or not, but if he was, I didn't want to make things worse for him.

I decided to call Mona. She and Dad had been married for a couple of years, and even though it hadn't worked out, we'd stayed in touch. She was as close to a mother as I had, or at least as I had before I was stuck with network TV.

Of course she was out too. It was Saturday night, and no one was home. Her answering machine made its standard beeps, and I tried to think of what I needed to say.

"Hi, Mona, it's Brooke," I said. It felt good just saying that and not Amy. "Uh, this is kind of complicated, but they had a show on tonight about missing people, and, well, I saw myself so I called the eight-hundred number, and now the police are here, and I'm supposed to go to the police station and meet a caseworker or something." It was a good thing Mona had a talk-as-long-as-you-want kind of message. "Anyway, the thing is Dad doesn't know, so if you could give him a call when you get in and tell him where I am, it would be a big help. Oh, it's ten of nine now. Saturday. Saturday night. Uh. Well, take care, and I'd still like to see you next weekend. I'm not getting arrested. Good-bye." I hung up. The policewoman was demonstrating her complete lack of interest in my message by looking through Charleen's videotape collection. I hoped she'd watch her step. There were two egg yolks right behind her.

"I found someone," the policeman said. "Mrs. Cobb three doors down. She's coming right over."

Where was Mrs. Cobb this afternoon when we needed her?
I thought. If she'd agreed to baby-sit in the first place,
none of this would be happening.

Mrs. Cobb was clearly no stranger to Brian and Tiffany. She came armed with a baseball bat. "When's the
tramp coming back?" she asked me.

"Probably not until tomorrow morning," I said.

"Then pay me now," she said. "Twenty bucks, or I'm
out of here."

"I don't know if I have twenty bucks," I said. I
checked my pocketbook, and all I had was a ten and two
singles. "Sorry," I said. "This is it."

"I'm not risking my life for no lousy twelve bucks,"
Mrs. Cobb said.

"You have a five?" the policewoman asked her partner.

"Do I have to?" he asked.

"Yes," she said. "Here, Mrs. Cobb. Here's a five
from me and a five from my partner. Now, give Amy her
two dollars, and we're settled here."

"Okay," Mrs. Cobb said. "You got any messages for
the tramp when she comes back? Like why you got arrested?"

"I'm not arrested," I said. What I was was furious.
Not only hadn't I been paid for staying with those monsters but I was now out ten bucks. If this wasn't the worst
night of my life, I shuddered to think what the competition would be like.

The officers waited for me to get my bag and my
jacket, and then we walked to the squad car together. It

didn't matter that I wasn't being arrested. I certainly felt like I was, like I was guilty of every unsolved murder in America. I would have confessed to shooting JFK if they'd asked me.

Charleen lived about five blocks away from the police station, so the drive was short and free of small talk. I wondered exactly how Mona was going to tell Dad, and for that matter when. At that point all I wanted was to be sent home. I could give Mrs. Girard a call in the morning, after we'd all had a good night's sleep. She'd waited eleven years, she could wait another night.

I knew I shouldn't think of her as Mrs. Girard. I tried remembering what I'd called her when I was little, but it was hard. First Dad had told me she was dead, and I know I cried a lot then, and he would hold me and say things were going to be okay. Then I found out she wasn't dead, and he told me why he'd taken me, how bad she'd been, and how he'd taken me to save me from her. He cried then, and it was my turn to hold him. Between the two, thinking she was dead and thinking she was bad, I hadn't thought very much about her. It just made me hurt when I did. I wasn't sure what I'd called her. Mommy probably. That's what Tiffany called Charleen.

I was sixteen years old. There had to be something between "Mommy" and "Mrs. Girard" that I could call her.

"We're here," the policeman said. "Sal, you take her in. I'll meet you there in a minute."

"Okay," she said. "Come on, Amy. This shouldn't take too long."

I nodded and followed her into the station. We'd gone on a class trip when I was in second grade to a police station, but that was in a different town. Dad and I moved around a lot the first couple of years. But this police station looked like what I remembered. Big and cold and scary. Or maybe I just felt small and cold and scared.

"I'm Mrs. Markowitz," a woman said, walking over to us. "You must be Amy?"

I nodded.

She smiled at me, and for the first time that evening I felt like crying. "I'll take over now," Mrs. Markowitz said to the policewoman. "Thank you."

"It's okay," the policewoman said. "I only wish all our calls were for happy stuff like this."

"Sit here with me, Amy," Mrs. Markowitz said. She found an empty bench and gestured for me to join her. "This must be very confusing for you."

"Uh, yeah," I said. I closed my eyes hard and willed myself not to start bawling. One tear fell, but I wiped it away fast. Two heavy swallows, and I was okay.

"The people at *Still Missing* called us as soon as you called them," Mrs. Markowitz said. "They also called your mother, naturally enough. She'd like to talk to you. I have her number."

"Do I have to?" I asked. "Couldn't it wait?"

Mrs. Markowitz smiled at me. "It would mean a lot to her," she said. "She's scared none of this is real, that there's been a mistake and you're not really Amy."

"Maybe I'm not," I said, and for the first time I started to feel better. Amy Michelle was a pretty common combination of names, after all, and Dad wasn't the only guy in the world who looked like that with a mustache. "You're right. I should talk with her right now, just in case this is a mix-up." I felt giddy with relief. Not that Mrs. Girard hadn't seemed like a very nice woman. But I had Dad. I had Mona. I even had Charleen. I could do just fine without a Mrs. Girard.

"We can use this office," Mrs. Markowitz said. "Come with me, Amy."

"Call me Brooke," I said. Just because I'd been Amy in a previous lifetime didn't mean I had to answer to it now. Not when the real Amy Michelle Donovan was still missing, in spite of *Still Missing*. It was all I could do to keep from laughing out loud.

Mrs. Markowitz took a slip of paper out of her pocket and dialed a number. "Hello, Mrs. Girard?" she said. "I have the girl here. Yes, she's willing to speak with you. Hold on." She handed the phone to me.

"Hello," I said.

"Hello," she said. She sounded as scared as me.

"This is really pretty weird," I said, and she laughed.

"Very weird," she said. "I've dreamed about this moment for so long, and now I don't know what to say."

"Well, it occurred to me this might be a mistake," I said. "I mean, I guess my name was Amy Michelle once, but there are probably lots of Amy Michelles wandering around loose, and I'm real sorry if I'm not your daughter."

"But you live with your father, don't you?" she asked.

"Yeah," I said.

"And you have since you were five?" she asked.

"Five or six," I said. "I don't remember exactly when."

"Do you remember anything about your mother?" she asked. "Anything about your life before your father kidnapped you?"

"He didn't kidnap me," I said. "He's my father. Fathers don't kidnap."

"Before he took you," Mrs. Girard said. "What do you remember?"

Mrs. Markowitz didn't have Charleen's video collection to pretend to look at, so she just sat there staring at a calendar. "What do I remember?" I said. "Not a lot."

"Maybe you had a dog," Mrs. Girard said. "Do you remember a dog?"

I tried to pretend I wasn't in a police station with a caseworker sitting by my side. I was five years old. Mona worked at a summer camp that specialized in the arts, and I went there summers and we did acting exercises. I tried to recapture the fiveness in me, and I felt an overwhelming urge to suck my thumb.

"I sucked my thumb," I said. It was funny how I could remember that so vividly. Maybe because it seemed like such a comforting thing to do just then. "Every night. Mommy didn't want me to, but my new daddy said it was probably because of the baby. There was a baby. I wanted a baby brother, but it was a girl instead, and I cried, and my new daddy said little sisters were great, but if I really really wanted, he'd see about trading the baby for a little

23

brother, and I knew this was like the most important thing I'd ever have to decide, and I was scared, and I thought how sad Mommy would be if I made her trade, so I said we could keep her. And my new daddy gave me a big hug and said I'd done the right thing, and I was going to be the best big sister in the world. But I don't remember a dog."

Mrs. Girard was crying.

"I'm sorry," I said. "Did you have a dog? I think I remember a cat."

A man got on the phone. "This is Mike Girard," he said. "I've been listening in on the extension."

"Hi," I said. "I'm sorry if I upset her. I guess I'm not Amy. Your Amy, I mean. I don't remember a dog."

"There wasn't one," he said. "But there was a cat, and you did suck your thumb, and I did offer to trade for a little brother."

"Oh," I said.

"I don't believe this," he said.

"I'm sorry," I said. "I didn't mean to be such a bother."

"This is no bother," he said. "Look, your mother and I will be driving to Windsor right away. If we drive straight through, we should be there by tomorrow morning."

"There's no rush," I said. "Why don't you get a good night's sleep and come on up tomorrow?"

"Neither one of us will be able to sleep," Mr. Girard said. "Let me speak to the caseworker, all right?"

"Sure," I said, delighted to get off the phone. Mrs. Girard hadn't stopped crying.

"Don't worry, arrangements have been made," Mrs. Markowitz said. "Yes, tomorrow morning will be fine. I'll be waiting for you at my office, and we can proceed from there. Yes, she's obviously all right. Yes, I will." She handed the phone over to me. "Your mother wants to say something to you," she told me.

"Yeah, hi," I said into the phone.

Mrs. Girard was still sniffling. "I love you, Amy," she said. "I've told you that every morning and every night since you've been missing. And tomorrow morning I'll get to tell you that in person."

"Uh, thank you," I said. "I mean, for loving me. I mean, I guess I'll see you tomorrow." I no longer knew just what I meant, and I hung up the phone fast before anybody asked for explanations.

"They're driving up tonight," I said to Mrs. Markowitz. "They won't get here before morning. So how about if I go home and spend the night there, and tomorrow we can all get together somewhere? We could have breakfast together. Okay?"

"I'm sorry, Amy," Mrs. Markowitz said.

"Brooke," I said. "My name is Brooke."

"Brooke," she said. "But I'm afraid you can't go home."

"Oh, it's okay," I said. "Even if Dad isn't there. I'm sixteen. I can be left by myself. Besides, he'll show up soon enough. I could probably track him down if I really had to. You can leave me alone there, until he gets home."

"It's not that simple," Mrs. Markowitz said. "Brooke, your father abducted you. He broke the law."

"Yeah, I guess," I said. "But he didn't mean to."

"I know this is very upsetting for you," Mrs. Markowitz said. "But you have to understand something. Your father never had legal custody of you. No matter how many years you've lived together, no matter how much he might love you and you love him, he had no right to take you and no right to keep you, and no right to prevent your mother from raising you."

"I understand what you're saying," I said, although I wasn't positive that I did. "And if I were like ten or eleven, then I could see where it would matter. But I'm sixteen. I'm a junior in high school. I've got a life. It'll be nice having a mother again, I guess. I'm real sorry for her, going through all that, and if she wants, I'll visit her. I never had a brother or sister before. It'll be fun getting to know them. But that's no reason why I can't go home now. I don't live that far from here. I can walk."

"Brooke, listen to me," Mrs. Markowitz said. "You have to understand this. Your father broke the law. He could be arrested. It is possible he'll go to prison. Your mother has full legal custody of you. It doesn't matter that you're sixteen. You're still a minor. She expects you to return home with her, and you will."

"Dad arrested?" I said. "For what? For raising me?"

"He had no legal right to take you," Mrs. Markowitz

said. "He kidnapped you as much as if he had been a stranger."

"But he isn't a stranger," I said. "He's my father. He bandaged my knees. He made me stick to a curfew. He . . ." I wasn't going to start crying. I made a fist and let my fingernails cut into my flesh. "He can't go to prison," I said. "I don't care who she thinks she is."

"She's your mother," Mrs. Markowitz said. "And she loves you very much."

"How can she love me?" I asked. "She doesn't even know me. I've spent more time with you than I have with her. You don't love me, do you?"

"I feel very sorry for you," Mrs. Markowitz said. "I know this must be extremely painful for you. But believe me, Brooke, it will all work out the way it's supposed to. The court awarded your mother custody for a reason. She loved you when you were a little girl, and she's never stopped loving you. She's done everything she could think of to try to find you. Think about that for a moment. For eleven years now she's never given up looking and dreaming of the day she would see you again."

"I don't mind seeing her," I said. "I don't mind visiting her. But I'm not going to live with her. That's crazy."

"It won't be your decision," Mrs. Markowitz said. "Monday morning you'll all go before a family-court judge, and this will get resolved then."

"You mean the judge could say I can keep on living right here?" I said. "With Dad?"

"It's possible," Mrs. Markowitz said. "But I don't think you should count on it, Brooke."

"But that's great," I said. "Will I get to talk to the judge?"

"I'm sure you will," Mrs. Markowitz said.

"Then I'll just explain the situation," I said. "How well I'm doing in school. How Dad and I look out for each other. The judge'll understand. Why didn't you tell me about him sooner?"

"Brooke, you have to be prepared for what the judge decides," Mrs. Markowitz said.

"I'm prepared," I said. "Look, he'll probably make me spend my summer with them. The Girards. That's fine. I was going to work as a camp counselor, but that's no big deal. Mona'll understand. I bet she'll be glad for me, getting to spend time with my mother. She . . . well, you don't need to hear about all that. So what happens next?"

"I'm going to take you to a very nice home for you to spend the weekend," Mrs. Markowitz said. "Until the judge decides what's going on, you'll stay there."

"Why can't I just go home?" I asked.

"Because there's a risk your father will abduct you again," Mrs. Markowitz said. "And even if you want him to, he still has no legal right to do it."

"But he'll know where I am," I said.

Mrs. Markowitz shook her head. "He'll know you're in foster care," she said. "But not where. Tomorrow I'll arrange for a visit between you and your mother."

"No," I said. "If I can't see Dad, I'm not going to see her."

"Nobody's going to force you to," Mrs. Markowitz

said. "But I want you to think about it tonight, think how your mother will feel if you refuse to see her. Think about her eleven years of pain and longing, not knowing where you were, if you were even still alive."

"That's not fair," I said.

"What your father did wasn't fair," Mrs. Markowitz said. "Not to your mother, and not to you for that matter."

"Can I speak to him?" I asked.

Mrs. Markowitz nodded.

"I don't have any clothes with me," I said. "If I'm going to meet my mother, I should at least have a change of underwear."

"I'll bring you something tomorrow morning," Mrs. Markowitz said. "Come on, Brooke. This is going to be a long, hard weekend for you, but there's no point spending it at a police station."

"Okay," I said. What were my options? All I could hope for was a sensible judge to straighten this whole mess out on Monday.

3

The foster home I was taken to was actually run by someone I knew. Mr. and Mrs. Grant had a son who had graduated from high school the year before. He'd dated my friend Tracy, and I'd been to a party at the Grants' house. It was an unbelievable comfort to be taken someplace I'd been to before.

Mr. and Mrs. Grant were real nice to me once Mrs. Markowitz dropped me off. Part of what was so spooky about the whole business was how nice everybody was being, like I was some kind of pathetic victim instead of a bigmouthed jerk.

As soon as I had a chance, I begged Mrs. Grant to let me use her phone. She said of course I could.

I called Dad, figuring I could at least leave an explanation on the machine. Only he ended up answering the phone himself. "Brooke, thank God, are you all right?" he asked. "Charleen forgot something, so we went back to her place, and you were gone, and that neighbor of hers said the police took you away. What the hell happened?"

"It's complicated, Dad," I said. Mrs. Grant was letting me use the phone in her bedroom, and I'd closed the door, but it still felt odd talking about such private things in a basically public place. "And you're going to get really mad."

"Are you in jail?" he asked. "I called the police station, and they didn't know anything about you."

They thought I was Amy Donovan. "I haven't been arrested," I said. "But you might be. Actually you might want to skip town. I'd forgive you if you did."

"Why should I be arrested?" he asked. "Oh, God."

"It's my fault," I said. "It's totally my fault. I was watching this TV show about missing people, and they had me on it. Like I was missing. And I don't know, it was stupid of me, but I called the eight-hundred number, and the next thing I know, cops are there, taking me away. I'm in a foster home now, but the person you ought to call is Mrs. Markowitz. She said she's listed under Steve Markowitz. She can explain better than me what's going to happen next."

"Did you speak to her?" he asked. "Your mother?"

"A little bit," I said. "She cried."

"Can you tell me where you are?" he asked.

"No," I said. "They don't want you to know so you won't snatch me again. But I'm okay. I know the people I'm staying with, and they're real nice. Oh, I called Mona and left a message with her, so she has some idea what's going on. And Charleen owes me ten bucks. Her neighbor made me pay in advance for taking care of Brian and Tiffany."

"You're all right?" he asked.

"Yeah, I'm fine," I said. "Only, Dad, Mrs. Markowitz said you committed a crime, and they might arrest you, and she said my mother's had legal custody of me all this time, and they might make me live with her, and I'm really sorry. . . ." And finally I began to cry.

"It's okay, honey," he said. "It's not your fault. I'm going to call this Mrs. Markowitz and get an official report on what's going on. Maybe they'll let me see you tomorrow. Either way, call me as soon as you get up in the morning, okay? And don't sleep too late. I'm going to go crazy waiting for that call."

"I think you should call a lawyer too," I said, trying hard not to sob.

"I will," he said. "Honey, it's going to be all right. I guarantee it. Now, I want you to get a good night's sleep, and I'll talk to you first thing tomorrow morning. All right?"

"All right," I said. I hated getting off the phone, but I knew Dad had other calls to make, and they were important ones. "Daddy, I love you."

"I love you too," he said. "And this will all work out." He hung up real fast, but I could tell he was crying also.

Mrs. Grant showed me where I'd be sleeping. There weren't any other kids there just then, which made me feel better. She really couldn't have been nicer. She didn't ask any questions or anything, and she didn't act surprised when I said I wanted to go to bed at nine-thirty. It was amazing how my entire life had changed in less than an hour.

I didn't sleep real well, and by seven I gave up and got out of bed. Mrs. Girard was just going to meet me with bags under my eyes. The Grants were still asleep, so I used the kitchen phone to call Dad. Ordinarily he's never up by seven on a Sunday, but this was no ordinary Sunday.

"You okay?" he asked after he picked up the phone on the first ring.

"I'm fine," I said. "Do you know what's happening?"

"Mrs. Markowitz told me everything she could," he said. "Your mother and her husband are driving into town today, and apparently they can see you even if I can't. But not at your foster home. Mrs. Markowitz will pick you up and take you someplace to meet them. I want you to behave yourself when you're with them, Brooke. No talking back. No tantrums."

"But if I'm rotten to them, maybe they'll decide they don't want me after all," I said.

Dad was silent for a moment. I knew him so well, I could picture exactly how he was rubbing his finger on his thumbnail. "Listen to me," he said. "This is very important and I don't know if we're going to have another chance to talk in private."

"Okay," I said.

"I am in deep shit," he said. "And my fate is pretty much in your mother's hands. If they think what I did was wrong but at least I did a good job raising you, they're a lot more likely to go easy on me than if they think I've abused you or turned you into some kind of monster."

"What does 'go easy' mean?" I asked. "You aren't going to have to go to jail, are you?"

"I hope not," Dad said. "And I hate to do this to you, but an awful lot is riding on your shoulders."

"So if I make them mad at me, they might take it out on you," I said.

"And you," he said. "Look, I talked to a lawyer last night, and to Mona. She sends her love, by the way. Nobody thinks I'll be allowed to . . . it's not very likely they'll let us stay together. The odds are you'll go live with your mother, the way you were supposed to all these years. Okay? That really shouldn't be too bad. It's good for a girl to know her mother. And, well, she had many fine traits. Many. It'll be nice for you."

"I don't want to live with her," I said. "I want to live with you, just the way we have been."

He ignored me. "The problem is if they think you're really troubled, or if you make things hell on your mother, then they won't send you back here," he said. "They'll make you a ward of the court, and you'll end up in foster care or in some institution somewhere, and, baby, that'll kill me, because it'll all be my fault, and there won't be a damned thing I can do about it. Do you understand?"

I wasn't going to cry again. I'd cried enough last night for a week, and I knew Dad had also. "I'll be good," I said. "I'll make her like me."

He laughed. It wasn't much of a laugh, but it was all he had to offer. "She's going to love you," he said. "And she's going to be proud of you, the same way I am. And really, no matter what, it isn't for too much longer. You'll be eighteen pretty soon, and then nobody'll be able to tell you what to do. And it'll be good. You'll have two sets of parents then, your mother and me, and her husband, and you know how much Mona loves you, you'll always have her. It's going to work out. It's what's right. It was wrong of me to take you the way I did, but I didn't trust the courts to give me custody, and I really felt I had to get you away from there, but that doesn't matter right now. That was eleven years ago, and God knows I've changed plenty in the past eleven years, and your mother has too, and what's important is you give her a chance. All she wants to do is love you. She . . . she's entitled. I was wrong, and she's entitled, and you're going to be the better for it. I mean that, Brooke. No matter what you think now, no matter what happens to me even, you're going to be the better for it."

"Yeah," I said. "That's what you said about braces."

He laughed. "And look at your gorgeous teeth," he said. "Show them off, okay? They cost enough."

"I won't let them send you to jail," I said.

"That's not your responsibility," he said. "And, honey, I don't blame you for calling that number. Hell, I would have too, if it had been about me. Who could resist something like that?"

I could hear stirrings in the house. "I'd better get off," I said. "Daddy, I love you."

"I love you too," he said. "Now, behave yourself, and make me proud of you."

"I will," I said, and I hung up. I left the kitchen and

went back to the room I was staying in. I didn't think it was wrong of me to call Dad, but just in case it was, I didn't want anyone to know about it.

About an hour later Mrs. Grant knocked on my door to say that Mrs. Markowitz had called. I'd heard the phone ringing, but when you're staying in someone else's house, you don't automatically assume a call's about you. "She's going to pick you up in an hour," Mrs. Grant said. "And you and your family will have breakfast then."

For a moment I thought she meant Dad, since he'd been the only family I'd had for about as long as I could remember. But then I knew she meant the Girards. What the hell was I going to call them? I knew instinctively that my calling her Mrs. Girard wasn't going to do Dad any good.

I wanted to shower, but I didn't have any clothes, so I waited until Mrs. Markowitz showed up. She brought me my own clothes, so I knew she'd seen Dad. "Is he okay?" I asked.

"Naturally he's upset," Mrs. Markowitz said. "But it's obvious that he loves you and wants what's best for you."

I could have told her that. Instead I changed my clothes and prepared to meet my maker, in a manner of speaking.

Mrs. Markowitz and I got in her car. "I'm taking you to my place," she said. "Your mother wanted to see you for the first time someplace private, and I volunteered."

"That's very nice of you," I said.

"It's not ordinary procedure," she said. "But this

isn't exactly an ordinary situation. Your mother seems very nice. She and your stepfather took turns driving last night, and they arrived in town around five this morning. They got a little sleep when they got in, but naturally they're very tired and they're very keyed up. Your mother's waited for this moment for a long time, Brooke."

"Yeah, I know," I said.

"I'm sure your feelings are mixed," Mrs. Markowitz said. "And I don't want you to pretend you feel things you don't. But remember, Brooke, this is your mother. You loved her once very deeply. That kind of love can get buried, but it almost never really dies."

"I don't know what to call her," I said.

"Oh," Mrs. Markowitz said. "That could be a problem. What did you call her when you thought about her?"

"I tried not to think about her," I said. "It kind of hurt when I did. Don't tell anyone that, okay?"

"Okay," she said. "Do you think you could feel comfortable calling her Mom?"

I shook my head. "I've been trying," I said, "but she keeps coming out Mrs. Girard."

"Then do what I did with my mother-in-law," Mrs. Markowitz said. "I didn't call her anything for a year and a half. After that I knew what to call her."

"She won't mind?" I asked.

"She probably won't notice," Mrs. Markowitz replied. "And if she does, she'll talk to you about it. She isn't the enemy, Brooke. The biggest mistake you can make is to think of her that way."

"I know," I said. "Dad told me the same thing. I just wish I knew what to call her."

"Give it time," Mrs. Markowitz said. "Give this whole business time. Don't expect to love her right away, although you may surprise yourself and find that you do. Don't expect to feel at ease. Just keep in mind how much she loves you, and you'll be fine."

"I'll try," I said. I stared out the window. Mrs. Markowitz lived in a nicer neighborhood than Dad or Charleen or even the Grants. I liked the town I lived in, because it had a lot of different neighborhoods. If I went to live with my mother, I'd have a whole new town to deal with.

I pointed out to myself that Dad and I hadn't exactly sat still the past eleven years. I went to first grade in one school and second grade in another and third, now that I thought about it, someplace else. Fourth grade, Dad met Mona, and we stayed where we were for a long time. But by eighth grade the marriage was over, and we'd moved again, and in ninth grade we made our last move. That was a lot of different towns, a lot of different schools. I could handle it if they made me.

"This is it," Mrs. Markowitz said. "My house, I mean. Do you want me to go in with you?"

"Oh, yes," I said. "Isn't your husband around too?"

"He's away on a business trip," she said. "But I'll come in since you want. I won't stay too long though. This isn't my reunion."

Mine either, I thought. It belonged to some kid named Amy Michelle Donovan.

Mrs. Markowitz unlocked the door and showed me to her living room. There were the Girards, just Mr. and Mrs. I wondered which neighbor had taken care of their kids last night and if she'd charged as much as Mrs. Cobb.

I told myself I was being stupid, thinking about stuff like that when I was meeting my mother for the first time in years. I told myself I should be completely open to the emotions, let them flow into me. This was my mother, for heaven's sake. She'd given birth to me and changed my diapers and did whatever it was mothers did to little kids.

But the truth was, if I hadn't seen her on TV the night before, she would have been a total stranger to me. There was no sense of lightning striking. She was a pleasant-looking woman with a pleasant-looking husband, and she saw me and rushed to me, and I braced myself for the hug.

"Amy, Amy," she said. I don't know how she got the words out, she was squeezing me so hard. "Oh, my darling Amy."

I wanted to say, "Call me Brooke, Mrs. Girard," but I knew better. I didn't say anything. I knew it would help if I cried, but I couldn't even manage that. She must have thought she was hugging a log.

"Let me look at you," she said, which gave me the opportunity of inching ever so slightly away. It was a good thing I did, because when I stood real close to her, I couldn't breathe. "Oh, Amy, you're so grown up."

"I'm sixteen," I said.

"Fifteen," she said.

"Sixteen," I said. Maybe I was the wrong Amy after

all. Lots of Amys probably told their stepfathers not to bother trading babies.

"Your birthday is in two weeks," she said. "April thirteen."

"My birthday was in October," I said. "October the eighteenth. I had a party."

"I don't believe this," she said. "It isn't bad enough all he did to us. He even changed her birthday. What grade are you in?"

"I'm a junior," I said.

"You should be a sophomore," she said. "I bet you never went to kindergarten, did you?"

"No," I said. "Daddy said I was so smart, I could start in first grade."

"He did it deliberately," she said. "To make it harder for us to find her. That bastard. I'd like to kill him."

"Now, Mrs. Girard," Mrs. Markowitz said. "I know this is very stressful for you. Why don't we all go into the kitchen and have something to eat."

"Thank you," Mr. Girard said. "We're very tired. This has all been very hard on Betty."

"I'm sure it has been," Mrs. Markowitz said. "How about if I make us a cheese omelet? How does that sound?"

"Don't go to any bother," I said.

"It's no bother," Mrs. Markowitz said. "Just think how lucky you are, Br . . . Amy. You're going to turn sweet sixteen twice."

"Yeah," I said. "Great." Just what I needed, to be six months farther away from eighteen. I stared longingly at

Mrs. Markowitz as she went into the kitchen to start breakfast.

"You're very pretty, Amy," Mr. Girard said. "Isn't she, Betty?"

"She's beautiful," she said. "I used to imagine what you looked like, and then with the computer picture I thought I had some idea, but you're much prettier than the computer made you out to be."

"Thank you," I said. I figured if all I said was thank you, I should be okay.

"And a junior already," Mr. Markowitz said. "I teach biology, you know. Did you take bio yet?"

"Last year," I said. "I liked it. Not enough to be a doctor or anything, but I liked it."

"What do you like best in school?" he asked.

"English," I said. "And history. Uh, what do"—what the hell were their names?—"what do Holly and Timmy like best?" "Timmy" almost came out "Tiffany."

"Holly's a scientist, just like me," Mr. Girard said. "And Timmy's favorite subject is recess."

I laughed. Not too hard, but a little, and even that helped. "That was my favorite in fourth grade too," I said.

"Timmy's in third grade," my mother said.

"Oh," I said. "He seemed very mature for his age. On TV last night, that is."

"That must have been quite a shock for you, seeing yourself like that," Mr. Girard said. "We were wondering, did you have any idea of what your mother had been through all these years looking for you?"

"Uh, no, not exactly," I said.

"Just what lies did your father tell you?" my mother asked.

"I don't know," I said. "I don't remember exactly."

"Betty," Mr. Girard said.

"I'm sorry," she said. "Amy, I really am. I've just had so many fantasies about this moment, and now that it's finally here, I'm exhausted and I feel so strange, and I don't know any of the right things to say."

For the first time I liked her. "I don't know what to say either," I said. "Except I wish you wouldn't say bad stuff about my father. I know you're really angry and you must hate him a lot, but I don't. I love him, and when you say bad things, I don't know what to do."

She took a deep breath. "You're absolutely right," she said. "This is no time for anger. This should be the happiest day of my life."

"I, uh, I got kind of confused about something last night," I said. "Do you have a dog?"

Mr. Girard laughed. "There's no dog," he said. "We were afraid we might get some cranks claiming to be Amy, to be you, so we decided we'd ask them if they remembered a dog. If they said yes, we'd know they weren't really Amy."

"That's pretty sneaky," I said. Dammit, why hadn't I remembered a dog? One nostalgic ode to Spot, and I wouldn't be in this jam.

"For all we know, we got other calls," Mr. Girard said. "Although probably not. *Still Missing* said they'd screen things first, and I'd say they did an excellent job."

"Breakfast is ready!" Mrs. Markowitz called from the kitchen. My mother and I followed Mr. Girard to the table.

"Help yourselves to coffee," Mrs. Markowitz said. I made sure to wait until everybody else had poured themselves some before I took any.

"You drink coffee?" my mother asked.

"Sure," I said.

"Betty," Mr. Girard said.

I figured that had to be their code to keep her from going crazy. I wasn't sure how bad it was that I drank coffee, but then again, just a few minutes before, I'd been sixteen.

"This is a very nice kitchen," Mr. Girard said to Mrs. Markowitz. "Do you do much cooking?"

"Not as much as I'd like," she said. "My husband likes to cook too. We have friends over for dinner once or twice a month."

"That's nice," he said. "Betty and I don't do nearly as much socializing as we'd like."

"We haven't really had the money for it," my mother said. "There've been a lot of expenses looking for Amy."

Great. If they expected me to pay them back, Charleen had better hand me over my ten bucks.

"And of course Holly and Timmy keep us quite busy," Mr. Girard said. "Do you have any children, Mrs. Markowitz?"

"No, not yet," Mrs. Markowitz replied. "My husband and I are trying to adopt."

I considered offering her me. It seemed like a great

compromise. And at this point she knew me a whole hell of a lot better than my mother did.

Mr. Girard sipped his coffee. My mother nibbled at her omelet. Mrs. Markowitz pretended like this was the way she always spent her Sunday mornings.

"So, Amy," Mr. Girard said. "You're a junior already. Have you been thinking about college?"

"Yes, sir," I said. I could call him sir and her ma'am and never have to worry about it. "Dad says he isn't sure how we'll find the money for it, but if I'm willing to work, we'll find a way."

"How are your grades?" he asked.

"B-plus, A-minus," I said. "I'm on the honor roll."

"That's great," he said. "I gather you like school."

"I do," I said. This was good, I knew it. He taught, and I liked school, and that had to help Dad. "I'm assistant news editor of *The Eagle*. That's the school paper." I realized that I'd be a story in the next issue, and nearly choked on my omelet.

"Maybe you'll major in journalism," he said. "That seems natural enough if you like English and history."

"She's fifteen," my mother said. "She doesn't have to decide what she's going to major in."

I lost my appetite. I hadn't had all that much of one to begin with. I put my fork down and tried not to look too sick.

"Maybe this will be easier on all of you if you get a little rest," Mrs. Markowitz said. "Why don't you go back to your motel and just stretch out for a while? If you fall asleep, fine. If not, just relax. I'm sure you'd feel better if you did."

"I want to be with my daughter," my mother said. "It's been eleven years. I don't want to take a nap. I want to talk to her and hold her and tell her how much I love her."

"I understand," Mrs. Markowitz said. "But this is very hard on Amy, and I think she could use the time to adjust."

"I'm okay," I said. "This is very exciting for me." I smiled to show how excited I was.

Mr. Girard looked at me and then he looked at his wife. "Betty, let's go back to the motel," he said. "Mrs. Markowitz is absolutely right. I, for one, am dead on my feet. And we want to call the kids and tell them all about their big sister."

"I'm scared," she said, and then she started to cry. "How do I know I won't lose her again?"

"You won't," I said. "I promise. I won't go anyplace I'm not supposed to. Hell, I want to get to know my mother. Mothers are good things. They love you and . . . and stuff like that."

"Come on, Betty," Mr. Girard said. "Let's get some rest. We have a long couple of days ahead of us."

"You promise you won't run away?" my mother asked me. She reached her hand out for mine, and I was forced to take it.

"I promise," I said. Not for her sake, but for Dad's.

"All right," she said.

"Do you think you can find your way back to the motel?" Mrs. Markowitz asked.

"I'll just reverse the directions," Mr. Girard said. "We'll do fine."

"Call me this afternoon," Mrs. Markowitz said. "When you're feeling more comfortable."

"We will," he said. "Come along, Betty."

I watched as the two of them left the house. My mother stood for a moment at the doorway, and I wasn't sure she was actually going to leave, but she did. I was fine until I heard the car start to drive away. Then I began to sob, harder than I had the night before, harder than I had when I'd learned my mother wasn't dead after all but just hadn't wanted me, harder than I knew a person could sob, and Mrs. Markowitz took me in her arms and let me sob as though I were her baby.

4

"The court proceeding isn't going to be like what you've seen on TV," Mrs. Markowitz told me the next morning as she drove me there. "Judge Kelly has agreed to meet in chambers. It'll be more like a conference than a trial."

"Will Dad have a lawyer?" I asked.

"Yes, he will," Mrs. Markowitz said. "Your mother will too. My understanding is the judge is going to speak to all of them individually and then tell them his decision as a group. He'll speak to you in private as well."

"That's good," I said. Private was the last thing I'd been the past couple of days. Even my second meeting with the Girards had been in public. We'd had dinner together the night before at the kind of restaurant Dad could never afford. It had gone better than breakfast, but I still wasn't comfortable with them. Still, I'd learned stuff. My mother worked in hospital administration. Holly dreamed of being an actress. Timmy played third base. And they'd learned more about me.

And now, after another sleepless night, it was time for yet another stranger to make sense of my life. By this point Mrs. Markowitz and I were practically best friends; we'd had thirty-six hours to bond.

Mrs. Markowitz gave me a pat on the hand as she parked her car. "Hang in there," she said. "You'll feel better about everything once the decision is made."

She was probably right. I couldn't feel worse. I followed her through the building, and once again I felt guilty of some unspecified crime.

The Girards were already in the waiting room when we arrived. I said hello to them, but I stuck by Mrs. Markowitz's side until Dad came in. As soon as I saw him, I rushed over, and we hugged each other hard. "You okay?" he asked me.

"I'm fine," I said. "I'm scared."

"Nothing bad is going to happen," he said. "I promise."

Dad had promised me a lot over the years, and he always came through. I would have stayed there by his side forever except that Mona entered. I hadn't known she'd be coming, and I was thrilled that she had. We embraced also.

"I'll do what I can," she whispered to me. "I don't have any legal rights, but I wanted to be here anyway."

"Thank you," I said.

She glanced at the Girards. "They look very nice," she said. "Don't hold it against them, what your father did."

"I'm trying not to," I said.

The judge's secretary came out then and saw we were all assembled. First the Girards were called in. I sat with

Dad and Mona while we waited. We didn't talk. Everything we had to say was too serious. But just seeing them made me feel more like myself, more like Brooke Eastman, than I had in days.

Then they were called in, first Dad and then, at her request, Mona. The Girards came out and sat with their lawyer, whispering. I didn't try to make out what they were saying, because I figured I'd be happier not knowing.

"Amy, will you come in, please," the secretary said to me.

I followed her in. Dad and Mona smiled at me as we changed places, but I still felt terrified.

There was a big conference table, with chairs enough for twelve, and the judge was wearing his robes, which didn't make me feel any better. He gestured for me to sit next to him, so I did. I told myself family-court judges had to be nice, that was part of the job requirement, and willed myself to stop shaking.

"It's nice to meet you, Amy," Judge Kelly said. "I've heard a lot about you."

I forced myself to look at him and smile.

"This must be very difficult for you," he said. "And I'm not sure I know how to make it easier. Why don't you start by telling me something about yourself?"

"I'm sixteen," I said. "Well, I was sixteen, only now it turns out I'm fifteen." I bit my lip.

Judge Kelly smiled. "You're a junior in high school, right?" he said.

"Yes," I said. "I am. And I'm on the honor roll, and I work on the school paper, and I used to take tuba lessons, because Dad heard that decent tuba players can always get scholarships to college, but I hated it, I really did, so he said I didn't have to keep playing. And I wanted to get a part-time job this year, you know, at Burger Bliss or someplace like that, and Dad said he'd think about it, and then he said he'd read up on it, and kids who had jobs were more likely to get into trouble, buy drugs and stuff like that, so he said no, I should spend the time on my schoolwork instead. He's always looking out for me that way."

"It can't be easy," Judge Kelly said. "Living alone with your father."

"As opposed to what?" I asked, and then I realized that might sound smart-alecky. "It's fine. I mean, it was fine when he and Mona were together too. I love Mona; it was like having a mother. . . ." Damn. Now he'd think I wanted to have a mother.

"Mrs. Eastman seems like a very nice woman," Judge Kelly said. "And it's obvious she loves you a lot."

"I love her too," I said. "And Dad's never tried to stop us from being close. I don't have a lot of family, the way other kids do, but I have enough. Honest."

"Do you do the cooking and cleaning?" Judge Kelly asked.

"Some of it," I said. "Some Dad does. Neither one of us is real fussy."

"What are your evenings like?" Judge Kelly asked. "Do you and your father do many things together?"

"He helps me with my schoolwork," I said. "He always has. And he likes to read a lot, and so do I, so lots of times we just keep things quiet. Some nights we watch TV or a movie. Or I talk to my friends on the phone. Dad let me have a phone in my bedroom for my fifteenth birthday. I don't know. It's a life, you know. I just live it."

"Does your father ever do things that make you angry?" the judge asked.

"Sure," I said. "He's my father. Of course he does. I wanted to go out on dates when I was fourteen, and he said I was too young and he wouldn't let me, and he won't let me learn how to drive until next year—we had a big fight over that—and I have a curfew, which I could live without. He makes rules, and when I don't like them, I get angry."

"Has he ever hit you?" Judge Kelly asked.

I was prepared for that one. "He did a couple of times when I was younger," I said. "A lot younger, like six or seven. And then he stopped. I asked him about that a couple of years ago. We'd been watching a movie on TV about child abuse, and I remembered how he'd hit me, and he said he'd been drinking too much and he was taking it out on me and it scared him, and he started going to AA, and he stopped drinking and he started reading books on how to be a good parent, and he still felt terrible shame at what he had done. I remember it because of that phrase, 'terrible shame.' When I went to bed that night, I thought about how lucky I was, how I had the best father in the world, because he didn't just hit me and feel bad. He felt bad and he made himself change."

"What has he told you about your mother?" the judge asked.

I'd spent a lot of the night thinking about how I was going to answer that question. "He told me she'd died," I said. "When I first starting living with him."

"How did that make you feel?"

"Sad," I said. "And scared. I'd never really lived with Daddy. But Daddy kept telling me how much he loved me and how it was going to be all right, and I believed him. And it was all right."

"Did he ever tell you your mother wasn't dead?" the judge asked.

"When I was eleven," I said.

"What exactly did he tell you?" the judge asked.

"He said he was sorry he'd lied to me," I said, carefully choosing which truths to tell him, "but I was old enough now to know the truth. He said my mother had problems, she drank, and she wasn't able to take care of me. He said she'd been beating me, he'd seen the bruises, and he felt the only way he could save me was by taking me away."

"Do you remember her hurting you?" Judge Kelly asked.

I shook my head. "But I don't remember it not happening either," I said. "I really think it could have happened that way. I don't know why else he would have taken me. Dad's very big on respecting rules."

"Do you feel angry at your father?" Judge Kelly asked. "For keeping you from your mother all these years."

"Absolutely not," I said.

"Really?" Judge Kelly said.

"Really," I said. "I love my father, and I like my life here, and sure, someday I'll be mad at him, but not now. He raised me. He bandaged my knees, and he went to all my band recitals, and he's gone without so I could have things. I don't know what kind of mother she is. But I do know I have the best dad in the world."

"Aren't you at all curious about what kind of mother she is?" the judge asked. "Now that you've finally met her."

"I'm sure she's a fine mother," I said. "She has two other kids, and I bet she does a great job with them. But she doesn't feel like a mother to me. Mona is mother enough for me. I don't need a mother. I never have. I don't even know what to call her, and I don't need her in my life. Things are just fine without her."

"But you called that eight-hundred number," the judge said. "You identified yourself as her missing child."

"Biggest mistake I ever made," I said. "I just did it, you know. It never occurred to me there'd be consequences. I thought, 'Well, look at that, they're talking about me,' and they kept showing that damned number on the bottom of the screen, so I called. I didn't even think, 'Well, now her mind will be at rest,' or 'Gee, it might be interesting meeting her.' I didn't think of anything. I just dialed, and the next thing I knew, there were police there, and I wasn't being allowed to see my father." I swallowed hard to keep from crying. "I'm sixteen," I said. "Okay, I'm not sixteen, but I will be in a couple of weeks, and I'm old enough to know what I want, and what I want is for my life to get back to normal. I want to be in school today. I have a big history test on Wednesday. I want to study for it. I want Jason Best to ask me out. I want to finish the book I'm reading. I want to sleep in my own bed tonight and know Dad is in his room, right next to mine. I want my life back, okay?"

The judge nodded. "I think I've heard enough," he said. "Miss Rossetti, will you call everybody back in here?"

I sat absolutely still. I wasn't one for praying—it was a good thing the judge hadn't asked about Dad and religion—but I slipped in a quick prayer that the judge would put my feelings first. It wasn't like they were unreasonable feelings. Who could blame me for wanting to stay Brooke Eastman?

Everyone came back in—the Girards, Dad, Mona, Mrs. Markowitz, both lawyers, Miss Rossetti. The conference room looked a lot smaller with all of us sitting around the table.

"This is not an easy moment," Judge Kelly said. "There are no simple answers. Irreparable harm has been done, and I cannot guarantee that this court, or even time itself, can right things."

Mrs. Girard was crying. Her husband held her hand. Dad was rubbing his fingernail at a furious pace, and Mona was staring at the judge. I knew that look. She was trying to will him to do what she wanted. It had never worked with me.

"There is no question, legal or moral, about custody," Judge Kelly said. "Elizabeth Girard has full legal custody of her daughter, Amy Donovan."

"No," I said.

The judge ignored me. "Amy will resume her life with the Girards immediately," he said. "When they leave for their home today, she will go with them."

Now Dad was crying.

"Your Honor," Mr. Girard said. "I don't know if it's our place to say this, or even if it's the right time, but my wife has decided not to press charges against Mr. Donovan. She has no desire to see him in prison."

The judge nodded. "That is very good of you," he said to her. "Mr. Donovan has lost all visitation rights. He will not be allowed to see Amy until she is eighteen."

"You can't do this," I said.

"He will not be allowed to call Amy," the judge continued. "If an emergency arises and contact must be made, he must inform the court, and the court will decide whether the call can be made. I cannot legally forbid him from writing, but any letters he writes or packages he sends to Amy, Mrs. Girard has the right to open and read."

"Your Honor, please," Mona said.

"If, after one year the Girards agree to it, Mr. Donovan may have a supervised visit with Amy, not to exceed one afternoon," the judge continued. "The place will be of the Girards' choosing, and there will be a court-appointed third party in constant supervision."

"I don't understand," I said. "Why are you hurting him like this?"

Judge Kelly looked right at me. "Your father has had eleven years with you to lie about your mother," he said.

"He has kept you from knowing her, from loving her, and from enjoying the gifts of her love. In two years you'll be eighteen and legally able to make your own decisions about where you want to live. That gives your mother two years, compared with eleven, to show you who she is, to show you who you are. The court cannot allow your father to interfere with that process. You say I'm punishing him. What the court is doing is freeing you from a decade of lies. You have a mother, you have a half sister and a half brother. You are a child now, although you may not feel that way. You won't be a child that much longer. While there's still a chance for you and your mother to develop the kind of relationship every daughter and mother are entitled to, you're going to take it. Amy, believe me, this is for your own good."

"I love my father," I said. "This isn't fair."

"Your father never gave you a chance," Judge Kelly said. "He's the one who's behaved unfairly."

"We'd like to take Amy home immediately," Mrs. Girard said. I was so angry, I couldn't even think of her as my mother anymore.

Judge Kelly nodded. "By all means," he said.

"What about my stuff?" I said. "My clothes. My things."

"You may go to your father's apartment and pack for your immediate needs," Judge Kelly said. "The court will see to it that the rest of your things are shipped to you."

"Can I be there?" Dad asked. "While she packs."

Judge Kelly paused for a moment. "Mrs. Markowitz,

would you mind supervising?" he asked. "Mr. Donovan is not to have any time alone with his daughter."

"Yes, Your Honor," Mrs. Markowitz said. "Come on, Amy. Let's go." She walked over to my chair and half pulled me up. I didn't mean to resist. I just didn't have the strength to stand.

"Your Honor, may I have contact with Brooke?" Mona asked. "I mean Amy."

"You may write to her," the judge said. "The Girards can decide if they want to permit greater contact."

"I hate you," I said. I said it at the judge, but I meant it for all of them.

Judge Kelly didn't seem to care. He sat there talking with the lawyers. Mrs. Markowitz put her arm around me, and we walked out together. Dad walked ahead of us, so I couldn't see his face.

I didn't say anything during the car ride home, and Mrs. Markowitz didn't try to make me feel better. She must have known she couldn't. I slammed her car door when we got to the apartment, as though this were her fault, and I hated it when she held me back, made sure I didn't get into the building first. We entered together, in stormy silence.

Dad was waiting for us. "I got out the big suitcase," he said. "And the duffel bag. I didn't think the judge would mind if you used both of them."

"That'll be fine," Mrs. Markowitz said. "Brooke, would you like help packing?"

"I don't need your help," I said. I went into my bedroom. Dad had left both the suitcase and the duffel on my bed. I stared at the chest of drawers and the closet. Compared with most of my friends, I didn't have that big a wardrobe, but I didn't see how I was expected to fit a life into two bags.

I took all my underwear first, threw it into the duffel, then my nightshirts and sweaters. The closet came next. I started with blouses and skirts, shirts and slacks. I began by folding them neatly, but after a while I just started slamming them into the suitcase. The couple of dresses I owned didn't fit. I got most of my shoes and sneakers into the duffel. I hadn't packed any of my books, my teddy bears, my jewelry. There was a picture of Dad, Mona, and me on my night table. I wasn't sure whether I was allowed to have it, so I buried it in my suitcase. If the Girards destroyed it, that was okay. Mona had a copy.

I grabbed my oldest teddy, a tiny bear Daddy had won for me at a county fair right before I'd started first grade. I had taken it to school with me, in my lunch box, for the first month or so. I needed it now just as badly. I went to the jewelry box next and threw its contents into the duffel. None of it was worth anything. What money we'd had had gone for tuba lessons.

"I'm finished," I said, having packed away eleven years in less than eleven minutes. I carried both bags into the living room.

"Mrs. Markowitz, I need to say good-bye to Brooke," Dad said.

She took a deep breath. "I can't leave the two of you," she said. "I'm very sorry."

"That's okay," he said. "Hell, by now the last thing Brooke and I have are secrets."

Fingers into fists. No tears.

"Brooke, you're a good girl," Dad said. "You have always made me very proud of you."

"Daddy," I said.

"No, let me finish," he said. "I don't think I can do this more than once."

"I love you, Daddy," I said. "I'm so sorry."

"You have nothing to be sorry about," he said. "The judge was right. I'm the one who did the wrong thing. I was scared, and I ran, and I hurt you. I never wanted to hurt you and I did."

"You didn't," I said. "You loved me."

"Oh, Brooke, you can love someone and hurt them anyway," he said. "The thing is, I'm very proud of you. You've never disappointed me, not about anything serious, and I know you're going to behave yourself now. You know right from wrong. You've always lived up to your responsibilities."

"I don't know if I can," I said.

"I know you can," he said. "Brooke, listen to me. I fucked up, and I did it big time. I was so scared of losing you. But I'm not scared anymore. It doesn't matter if we don't see each other for a year, for two years even. You're going to be my daughter until the day I die, and I'm going to be your father. I'll be at your . . . your college graduation, and I'll dance at your wedding, and I'll spoil your kids something rotten. Now, here's the ten bucks Charleen owes you, and another twenty besides. If you need anything, you let me know? And don't get any bright ideas about running back here. That'd be the biggest mistake you could make. The judge knows what he's doing. Do you have your bags? Is everything packed?"

"Daddy, please don't make me go," I cried. "Please."

"Just get out of here," he said. "I can't—"

Mrs. Markowitz grabbed my suitcase and my duffel with one hand and, with the other, pushed me away. I don't know how she did it. I don't know how Dad did it. I don't know how any of us did it, but we did.

5

Three hours into the drive I learned about my new high school. "You'll be going to Taylor High," Mr. Girard told me. "It's a good school, good academic program. About two thirds of its students go on to college."

"Is that where you teach?" I asked. It physically hurt to ask questions, like the inside of my throat had been rubbed raw with sandpaper.

"No, I teach at Oakdale, about a half hour away," he said. "That's also a good school, but a little smaller, more country. How big is the school you were going to?"

"About fifteen hundred," I said.

"Nine through twelve?" he asked.

I nodded. My mother was driving then, so he was looking at me.

"Taylor's about twelve hundred, also nine through twelve," he said. "So it's a little smaller than what you're used to."

"That's okay," I said.

"We went to your old school this morning," my

mother said. "We picked up your records. You certainly moved around a lot."

"I guess," I said.

"We were very impressed with your academic record," Mr. Girard said. "You never seem to have lost any ground, even with all those transfers."

"Dad worked with me," I said. "He always went over my homework with me."

"Oh," my mother said.

In the fourth hour, bedrooms came up.

"We've always lived in four-bedroom houses," my mother said. I'd been working very hard all afternoon at thinking of her that way. My mother. Sometimes it came out one word, mymother, and I still didn't feel any emotional connection—wow, that's my mother!—but it was better than calling her Mrs. Girard, even to myself. "So that when you came home, you'd have a room of your own."

"That's very nice of you," I said. "Thank you."

"You're my daughter," she said. "And I wanted you to be happy."

I didn't say anything.

"The problem is you can't keep a room empty very long," Mr. Girard said. "The fourth bedroom became a den quite a while ago. I have a lot of my stuff in there, and there's a sofa bed—the room doubles as a guest room when your grandparents come to visit."

"Tomorrow we'll go shopping for all new furniture," my mother said. "We'll turn it into the bedroom of your dreams."

"Oh, no, that isn't necessary," I said. "I don't mind sleeping on a sofa bed."

"Don't be silly," my mother said. "I've dreamed for years about what your bedroom would look like when you came home."

"But it isn't fair," I said. "Not to Holly and Tim. You shouldn't be doing stuff for me and not them."

My mother laughed. "Holly's been after me for months now to change her wallpaper," she said. "This is the perfect opportunity. And Timmy doesn't care."

"But where will . . ." Dammit, I couldn't call him Mr. Girard. "Where will all the other stuff go? The den stuff?"

"We've been talking about finishing the basement for years now," Mr. Girard said. "We finally have a reason to. Don't worry, Amy. Everything will fit into place eventually."

In the fifth hour I learned about rules.

"Your mother and I don't think of ourselves as being particularly strict," Mr. Girard said. "But we do have rules."

"Sure," I said.

"It may not seem fair to you, having to live by them, when you're used to, well, whatever," my mother said. "But the rules are for your own good."

"And of course we have Holly and Timmy to worry about," Mr. Girard said. "We can't have you following one set of rules when they're accustomed to another."

"Of course not," I said.

"The rules are really pretty basic," Mr. Girard said.

"No drugs. That includes cigarettes and alcohol. Home and away."

"We're not much for drinking," my mother said. "Sometimes at a party we'll have a little beer or wine, but that's about it."

"No sex," Mr. Girard said. "We don't know if you're a virgin, Amy, and frankly we're not going to ask. But as long as you live under our roof, you'll behave as though you are one."

"Of course you can date," my mother said. "We aren't going to treat you like a nun. But we will expect to meet any boy you want to go out with."

"You can understand how important these rules are because of Holly," Mr. Girard said. "She has a big sister now, and she's sure to be watching you, to see what she can get away with."

"No cursing," my mother said. "We couldn't help noticing that you do, Amy. Not that we fault you. But we try very hard to watch what we say in front of the children, and we'd appreciate it if you did the same."

"Okay," I said. I doubted I'd be saying very much for the next couple of years anyway.

"Those are the big three," Mr. Girard said. "We go to church on Sunday, and of course we'd appreciate it if you went with us."

"The church has a wonderful youth group," my mother said. "You could meet a lot of really nice boys and girls there."

"We'll work out a curfew for you," Mr. Girard said.

"And an allowance. Not every decision has to be made this minute."

"I don't need an allowance," I said, although I was damned if I knew where I was going to get money any other way. Darned. I was darned if I knew.

"Of course we'll give you an allowance," my mother said.

"You'll have some chores to do around the house as well," Mr. Girard said. "We all pitch in with the housework, even Timmy."

"We pick up after ourselves," my mother said. "Make our own beds, keep our rooms neat. Do you know how to vacuum?"

"Sure," I said.

"Maybe you'll do that," my mother said. "That might be a good chore for you."

"I don't care," I said. "Whatever."

"We'll decide after you're more settled in," Mr. Girard said. "Is there something around the house you enjoy doing?"

Watching TV. "I can pretty much do anything," I said. "Dad, well, we just shared the work. Whatever you want me to do is fine with me."

"Great," Mr. Girard said. "We'll find something for you to do."

Six hours into the trip I got the "I can never replace your father" speech.

"I can never replace your father," Mr. Girard said. "And I'm not going to try. But whether you remember or not, I lived with you and your mother for a year before you were kidnapped. Do you remember anything about that year?"

"Not much," I said. "Except the part about the baby being a girl."

He laughed. "That's one of my favorite memories too," he said. "You know, you were just starting to call me Daddy when he abducted you. I wanted to adopt you. I loved you just as much as I loved Holly."

"Thank you," I said.

"You were a precious little girl," my mother said. "So bright, so loving."

"I don't expect you to call me Dad," Mr. Girard said. "And I certainly don't expect you to call me Daddy. Do you know what you'd feel most comfortable calling me?"

Mr. Girard. "I haven't really thought about it," I said.

"How about if you call me Mike to begin with?" he said. "Later on if you want to call me Dad, well, it would certainly make me feel proud."

"Mike," I said. "Thank you." I hoped beyond hope my mother might offer me the Betty option, but she kept her mouth shut. Oh well. At least I had something to call him.

About half an hour before we reached their home, I was told what to expect.

"I guess we'd better warn you," Mike said. "About what to expect when we get home."

"You mean besides the sofa bed?" I asked.

He laughed. "That's the least of it, I'm afraid."

"You see, one of the conditions of *Still Missing* featuring us was they'd get exclusive TV rights to our reunion," my mother said.

"I don't remember any TV cameras," I said. "Back at Mrs. Markowitz's."

"We were able to persuade them not to show up," Mike said. "But in exchange for that they've insisted on being at the house when we get there."

"We know you're tired," my mother said. "And we're really sorry about this. But we had to get on the show. The competition is fierce, and they don't usually feature parental abductions."

"Luckily for us the producer's mother was hospitalized where Betty works," Mike said. "One of the nurses made the connection, so we had a great in."

"But even so, there were terms we had to agree to," my mother said. "It was desperately important to us to get on that show. You can understand why. It worked. If we hadn't been on, you'd still be a prisoner, and I . . ." She started crying. Fortunately Mike was driving.

"Anyway, we told them they couldn't shoot anything until the judge made his ruling," Mike said. "And they were pretty understanding. But they're going to be waiting for us when we get home. They'll show the reunion on Saturday's show."

"They're very excited," my mother said. "They don't usually have such fast results. It's great publicity for them."

I will never call an eight-hundred number again.

"The local paper'll be there also," Mike said.

"They've been covering the story ever since *Still Missing* agreed to have us on."

"I hadn't realized I was so newsworthy," I said.

"It's a small town," Mike said. "Something like this, a story with a happy ending, it's always big news in a town like that."

"That's great," I said. "They're not going to, like, interview me, are they?"

"They'll ask you a couple of questions," Mike said. "Don't worry, Amy. We'll see to it they don't stay too long."

"Fine," I said. Fine, great. What was I supposed to say? I'm thrilled at such a big turnout for my execution? I only hoped Dad didn't watch *Still Missing* on Saturday. I certainly wasn't going to.

The whole block was lit up when we finally got there, partly from the TV lights, but also all the houses had their outdoor lights on as well. There were balloons hung from streetlamps, yellow ribbons tied to all the trees, and a giant WELCOME HOME, AMY! streamer attached to the front of the Girards' house. Everybody was standing there, and when Mike and my mother got out of the car, people cheered.

I had sworn the Girards would never see me cry, and it was a good thing I'd vowed that to myself, because otherwise I don't think I could have made it out. All this is for Amy Donovan, I told myself, and I'm Brooke Eastman, and it doesn't count. It doesn't mean anything to me. I'm no more Amy Donovan than I am Scarlett O'Hara. I can do it. I am never going to cry again. I may have blinked a few times when I left the sanctuary of the car, but that was because of the TV lights. They weren't real tears. Not from my eyes, they weren't.

"Look this way, Amy," people said to me, and I did, and flashes went off. A TV camera followed the Girards and me as we walked toward the house. Holly and Timmy ran out. Timmy went to his mother, and Holly to her father.

"Kids, this is your sister," Mike said. "Finally you're getting to meet your sister." He was crying, and so was my mother, and so were half the people who lived on the block. I wasn't crying, though, and neither was Holly. Her father gave her a little shove, and she walked over to me and kind of hugged me.

Tim came over next. He held his hand out, like he didn't know what to do with it, so I shook it. Cameras flashed. People laughed. I actually felt sorrier for the kid than I did for me. I liked Tim from that moment on.

"Amy, how do you feel?" a man with a microphone asked. "Is this as exciting as you always dreamed it would be?"

"It's great," I said. "It's just amazing."

"After eleven years had you given up all hope of ever seeing your mother again?" he asked.

"I hadn't . . . Yes," I said. "I never thought we'd find each other."

"What did you think when you saw yourself on *Still Missing*?" he asked. He certainly was a persistent son of a . . . son of a gun.

"I thought, 'Is that really my mother?' " I said. Amy

said. Amy would know what to say. "I just couldn't believe it."

"And when you first saw her, after eleven years, what were the first words you said?" he asked.

I couldn't even remember. It had been thirty-six hours ago, and nowadays thirty-six hours was a lifetime. "I don't remember," I said. "I just remember hugging her."

"You have eleven years' worth of hugs stored up, don't you, Amy," he said. "Eleven long, lonely, motherless years to make up for. Betty! Betty, tell us what your first thought was when you saw Amy."

I might have listened to what she had to say except a newspaper reporter grabbed me next. "Is this the most wonderful moment in your life?" she asked. "This reunion with your mother?"

I tried to think what the competition was. I'd really liked my life, but it didn't seem to be wonderful moment followed by wonderful moment. How did meeting my mother compare with not having to take tuba lessons anymore? "This is great," I said. "The way the whole neighborhood showed up. I can't get over it."

"What are your plans for tomorrow?" the reporter asked.

"I guess I'll be starting school," I said. "Mike, Mr. Girard, my stepfather, well, he says Taylor is a really great school."

"You're a sophomore?" the reporter asked.

"Junior," I said. I didn't bother telling her I was going to turn sixteen again in a couple of weeks.

"Did your father mistreat you?" the reporter asked. "All those years he held you captive."

"No," I said. "My . . . he . . . I was fine."

"Did he apologize to you?" the reporter persisted. "When you finally learned the truth, did he tell you he was sorry?"

"I have a headache," I said. "The lights are so bright. I think I'll go inside now." I broke away from the reporter and plowed through the crowd into the Girard house.

There was no privacy there either. TV cameras had been set up. The Girards and the *Still Missing* people followed me in.

"Come on, everybody, get together," one of the TV people said. The Girards gathered together, and I joined them.

"A happy family, united at last," the *Still Missing* reporter said. "Amy, give your mother a kiss."

I hated the thought of even touching her just then, but I forced myself to put my lips on her cheek. I could taste her tears.

"Kids, why don't you show Amy her room," Mike said.

"Okay," Tim said. "Come on, Holly."

"I'm coming," she said. "It's this way." She pointed to the staircase in the hallway.

"Home at last," the TV man said. "A dream come true for Amy Donovan."

At least the camera didn't follow us upstairs. Holly and Tim went up first, and I followed them. They took me to what was obviously a well-used den.

"This is your room," Holly said.

"Great," I said. "It's very nice."

"You gonna get a real bed?" Tim asked.

"I think so," I said. "I don't care."

Holly stared at me. "How do we know you really are Amy?" she asked. "Maybe you're a fake. Maybe you're just trying to fool Mom and Dad so you can get all of their money."

I only wish. "They recognized my father," I said. "So I must really be Amy."

"Your father is a bad man," Tim said. "Your father is the worst man in the whole world."

"No, he isn't," I said.

"He is too," Tim said. "Isn't he, Holly?"

Holly nodded. "He's a terrible, awful man," she said. "My parents hate him. He's the worst man ever."

"Maybe they used to hate him," I said. "But I don't think they hate him anymore."

"They'll always hate him," Holly said. "We hate him too, don't we, Timmy?"

"He made Mommy cry," Tim said.

"Every Christmas," Holly said. "And in April, on Amy's birthday, and sometimes for no reason, she'd cry, and it was because of him. It's your fault too."

"My fault?" I asked. Just what I needed.

"You could have found us," Holly said. "You didn't want to. You wanted to stay with that bad man instead."

"You made Mommy cry," Tim said.

"I'm sorry," I said. "I didn't remember your name. I didn't know how to get in touch with you."

"Your father knew our name," Holly said. "I bet you never asked him."

She was right about that. "I feel sick," I said. "I think I may throw up."

"The bathroom's over there," Tim said. "You'd better throw up in there."

"Thank you," I said. I left the den and ran to the bathroom, slamming the door behind me. And for as long as it took to pretend I was vomiting, I had, if not peace, then a little privacy. A moment to be Brooke Eastman again.

6

My mother took me to the high school the next morning to register me for my classes. I sat in the office while she spoke to the guidance counselor. Kids came in and stared at me. I couldn't blame them. I'd been the front-page photo in the local paper that morning, with full-length coverage (and additional pictures) on page three. The whole story was there. Wicked father. Heartbroken mother. Innocent child. Deceit. Treachery. Imaginary birthdays. Eight-hundred numbers. I would have loved it if it hadn't been me.

Eventually my mother came out with the guidance counselor. Something about being home had changed my mother. She'd stopped crying and was smiling all the time instead. I wondered if she was more like the girl my father had fallen in love with so many years before, if this is what she would have been like if he hadn't taken me. There's a lot to wonder about when you're getting to know your mother.

"Mrs. Hendly will give you your schedule and show you around," my mother said. "They couldn't put you in honors classes, but if you do well enough this year, you'll be in the honors track next year."

"Great," I said. "Thank you." I felt the words tattoo themselves permanently on my forehead. *Great. Thank you.* I'd said them often enough.

"I'm going now," my mother said. "But I'll meet you here at the end of the school day so we can go furniture shopping."

"You really don't have to," I said. "There's no rush. The sofa bed is fine."

"You should have your own room," my mother said. "You're home now, and your room should be just the way you want it."

"I love shopping with my daughter," Mrs. Hendly said. "When she lets me."

"Holly's reaching that stage," my mother said. "They're so much smarter than their mothers sometimes."

Mrs. Hendly laughed. My mother laughed. I smiled to be polite. Mona and I had gone shopping together, and I'd been so happy to go with a woman, it never occurred to me to protest. Another stage I'd been deprived of.

"School ends at ten of three," my mother said. "I'll meet you outside at the main entrance. All right, Amy?"

"Sure," I said. Fine. Great. Thank you.

"I can't bear to leave her," my mother said to Mrs. Hendly. "I checked on her three times last night, just peeked in to see if she was all right. It was like having a newborn in the house."

"It's wonderful," Mrs. Hendly said. "It's a wonderful story. We're all so excited for you."

"Okay, I'll go," my mother said. "Ten of three at the main entrance. Good-bye, Amy." She paused for a moment and then kissed me. "Have a good day, honey," she said. "I'll see you later. And think about dream rooms."

"I will," I said.

Mrs. Hendly gave me a walking tour of the school, which wasn't going to do me much good, although I pretended that I was committing the layout to memory. Then she dropped me off at History, which was my first class of the day. When the bell rang, I stumbled my way through the building until I found my French class. Then Gym, and English, and finally lunch.

I sat alone in the cafeteria, counting my change. Mike had given me a five-dollar bill, which more than covered the cost of lunch, but I needed change and lots of it. I laughed to myself. The one thing I'd had that week was change, and here I was looking for more.

I nibbled at my tuna-fish sandwich and felt everybody staring at me. They'd been looking at me all day. I was used to being the new kid, used to unfamiliar looks, but this one set the record. I was thinking about dimes and quarters when a boy and a girl sat down next to me.

"Do you mind if we join you?" the girl asked.

"I don't care," I said.

The boy smiled. "My name is Chris Quinn," he said. "And this is Jessica Haverling. And you're Amy Donovan."

"So they tell me," I said.

"We figured you must be feeling pretty lonely," Jessica said. "Lonely and conspicuous. It's an awful combination."

"I'm okay," I said. With my luck they were undercover reporters.

"We came over for a reason," Chris said.

"Sure," I said. "What?"

Jessica smiled at me. They both seemed nice. A little richer than I was used to, better dressed, but nothing snotty or mean about them. "You know," she said to Chris, "I still don't feel comfortable doing this."

"Okay, I'll handle it, then," he said. "Right now, unless I'm totally mistaken, you feel like a member of the Freak-of-the-Month Club."

I laughed. "You're not totally mistaken," I said. At least he was being honest with me.

"That's what we figured," Jessica said.

"What are you?" I asked. "Social workers? Members of the Good-Samaritan Club?"

Jessica and Chris laughed. "Not exactly," he said. "The thing is, there's this unofficial group of us Freaks of the Month. Jessica and I are members. I'm a charter member actually. We're kids who for one reason or another everybody at the school has stared at."

"Lonely and conspicuous," Jessica said. "Like you're the only naked one in the whole school."

"Come on, now," I said. "You've been through this?"

"Not the same story, no," Chris said. "We all have our own stories."

"Here's mine," Jessica said. She lowered her voice,

and I had to concentrate to really hear her. "My mother drinks. Well, lots of kids' mothers drink. My mother drinks all the time, but even that wouldn't qualify me. But this fall, at Open School Night, my mother showed up slobbering drunk. She made a pass at the assistant principal. She threw up in the Home Ec room. I'm not even taking Home Ec. I have no idea how she ended up there. They called a cab for her, and she refused to leave. I think you have the idea."

"Were you there?" I asked.

"I didn't have to be," Jessica said. "Believe me, it was all over school the next day. Everyone's parents were there, they all saw something. I thought I'd die. I mean, it wasn't like people thought my mother was normal, but there was something so public about it, and her doing it here, on my turf. I hated it, I hated her, and I hated the way everybody looked at me."

"So we recruited Jessica for the Freak-of-the-Month Club," Chris said. "Which is officially known as Teens in Crisis."

"You mean it's an official school club?" I asked.

"Not a school club," Jessica said. "If it met in school, we'd have to have a teacher sponsor. We meet Fridays after school at the Unitarian Church. They let us have a room."

"We meet on Fridays so we'll have the strength to get through the weekend," Chris said. "Weekends are always the hardest."

Weekends. I hadn't thought about next weekend yet, that stretch of time I'd have to spend with the Girards, pretending to be happy, as though I belonged there, in my brand-new dream bedroom. I was supposed to visit Mona this weekend. Mona, who I might never see again. I bit my lip so hard, I could taste the blood.

"You have to be recruited for the club," Jessica said. "But when we heard about you, we all agreed you should be invited. Do you want to join us?"

"I don't know," I said. "How did this thing start?"

"I was one of the founders," Chris said. "Just about four years ago, freshman year, my father killed his wife."

"My God," I said.

"Not my mother," Chris said. "His third wife. My mother was his first wife. He'd left his second wife with a few bruises, but things got real bad with his third wife, and he beat her to death." He was silent for a moment. "She was pregnant," he said. "It was very bad."

It sure put my problems in perspective. "I can't imagine," I said.

"No, you can't," Chris said, and he smiled some more. "Not everybody realizes that. Thank you. Anyway, there I was fourteen years old, and my father was in jail, and everybody knew. I mean, it was all over the papers, TV, lots of coverage. My father is very rich. At least he was until he had to start paying lawyers to prove he was temporarily insane."

"Was he?" I asked.

"Unfortunately not in the eyes of the jury," Chris said. "Although they gave him the benefit of the doubt and said it wasn't premeditated. Which is good, because it means no death sentence. The point is everybody was staring at me, it felt like I couldn't breathe without people noticing, and I was going crazy at school. My mother tried to be helpful, she even offered to send me away, but I couldn't see the point. My father was going to be a murderer wherever I went, and I was either going to have to lie, which I didn't much want to do, or else people were going to find out. So I figured I'd stick it out here. That's when I got the idea for the Freak-of-the-Month Club. I knew I wasn't the only kid everybody was staring at. There were kids I'd stared at the month before. So I approached one of them. I won't tell you his story, but the gist of it is one of his parents had done something pretty awful and everyone knew. He was a junior, and he knew a girl, a senior, who people had been whispering about, and then there was another girl, also a freshman, who was involved in a really bad situation, and the four of us started the group."

"We have a rule about confidentiality," Jessica said. "What you hear at a meeting never goes any further. That's why Chris isn't telling you any of the details, except about himself. You can say anything you like at a meeting and never worry about anybody else hearing it."

"Anything?" I asked.

"Anything," Jessica said. "That's why there are no adult supervisors. It works out."

"We're not bad kids," Chris said. "None of us is about to assassinate the president."

"What about suicide?" I asked. I wasn't planning on it myself, but I was curious.

"One of the members killed herself last year," Chris

said. "We knew she was thinking about it. So did her parents, and her therapist. None of us could stop her. We tried as hard as they did."

"Usually when we recruit a member, we know about them," Jessica said. "They've been going to the school, we know their families, we certainly know their problems. That's the whole point. Everyone has problems. Ours are just a little more visible."

"So we're taking a chance asking you," Chris said. "All we know is what we read in the paper. And you may not fit in. You might drop out after a meeting or two. But we figured it wouldn't hurt to ask."

"What are the other rules?" I asked. "Is there a secret handshake?" I always wanted to belong to a club that had a secret handshake.

"I'm afraid not," he said. "The rules are pretty basic. You have to at least pretend to listen to what people are saying. No whispering, no passing notes. You can't tell people who else is in the club, but if you want, you can say you're a member. Only call it Teens in Crisis. It sounds more respectable that way."

"Is it like AA?" I asked.

Chris laughed. "We counted up once how many different Twelve Step groups we all were involved with," he said. "If you lined up all the steps end to end, you could climb to the top of the Empire State Building. We're not a Twelve Step group. No Higher Powers, nothing like that. It's just a place where you can unload."

"But you don't have to," Jessica said. "I didn't say a word my first three weeks there. It was just enough for me hearing what other people had to say. You know, when you're the one being talked about, you feel like nobody else in the world has problems, or if they do, they're nothing like yours. Just listening to what the other kids were going through made me feel less alone."

I had never felt so alone in my life. So alone and so exposed. Like I was the only naked one. "I'd like to join," I said. "Thank you for asking."

"Do you think you can make it until Friday?" Chris asked. "Is there something we can do in the meantime?"

"Are either of you juniors?" I asked. I would have loved to have someone whose name I knew to go to classes with me.

"I'm afraid not," Jessica said. "Chris is a senior, and I'm a sophomore. But there are kids in the group who are juniors. We'll send one over."

"Let me see your schedule," Chris said. I handed it over to him. He checked it out and nodded. "I know someone who's in that Chemistry section," he said. "I'll tell him to introduce himself."

"Thank you," I said. "I have a favor to ask. It's kind of an important one."

"What is it?" Jessica asked, and her willingness to do it was in her voice, her face.

"I need change," I said. "Lots of change. There's a pay phone there, I saw it, and I know . . ." No tears. No tears. "My father isn't home, but his machine'll be on, and I have to let him know I'm okay. He isn't allowed to call me."

Jessica opened her pocketbook, and Chris pulled out

all the change he had from his pockets. Between them they had seven quarters and five dimes.

"Stay here," Chris said. He left my table and started going from kid to kid.

"What's he telling them?" I asked.

"That he needs change," Jessica said. "Not why. Everyone knows Chris. They like him. They'll give him their change."

Sure enough, in five minutes he came back with two handfuls of change. "No pennies," he said. "But everything else people had."

"I have a ten," I said, handing it to him.

He shook his head. "It'd be too much bother figuring out who owes who money. Just take the change and make the call. The bell's going to ring pretty soon."

"Thank you," I said. "I will never forget this."

"It's okay," he said.

I poured the change into my pocketbook and watched as it flowed over my little teddy bear. I ran out of the cafeteria and over to the pay phone I'd spotted on the tour of the school.

It took almost all the change I'd been given to place the call, and at that I was only allowed one minute. I wasn't sure I could make it through when I heard the message, heard Dad's voice, and my own, reciting our phone number and giving the standard instructions.

"This is Brooke," I said real fast, so I could get it all in. "I'm at my new school. Everything is fine. The Girards are really nice. The trip was fine. I've met some really nice kids already. I'm great." *Fine, nice, great.* Was there any time left for the truth? "I love you, Daddy, and I miss you, but really I'm okay, and I just needed, well, I just needed to let you know. I'll write. I love you." I hung up. I hadn't cried. It had been twenty-five hours and ten minutes since I'd cried last. In twenty-five months I could cry all I wanted. That's all. Just twenty-five months to go.

7

My mother was waiting for me when I got out of school that day. I spotted her right away, but there was still no lurch of recognition. I'd been hoping there would be, that after a day away from her, a day spent in nightmarish confusion—Which class do I go to next? Why are they ahead of me in this subject, behind me in that?—the very sight of my mother would push me into Momhood, that feeling of being enveloped in love and protection that I knew from Dad. But there was nothing, just a sense of relief that I could pick her out of a crowd, not mistake her for a teacher or somebody else's mother. Oh well. It was a start.

"This is going to be so much fun," she said to me as we walked to her car. "I love shopping. Don't you?"

"Sure," I said.

"I can't wait to see what your taste is like," she said. "Whether we like the same things. Holly and I used to, but now she's at that stage where she has to decide for herself. Of course, the final decision will be yours. About your room, of course."

"Great," I said. "Fine."

"How was your school day?" she asked. "Confusing, I'll bet."

"It was okay," I said, rescued from *fine*ness. "The teachers seemed nice."

"Did you talk to any of the kids?" my mother asked. She started the car and maneuvered her way onto the street. "I bet they were excited to meet you. You're quite a celebrity in this town."

"A few of them talked to me," I said. "No one asked for my autograph."

"Wait until they see you on Saturday," my mother said. "No, I don't mean it that way. I know it must be awkward for you, having to make new friends and all."

"It's okay," I said. I really did feel sorry for her, having to make small talk with her daughter, not knowing what was safe to bring up. None of this was her fault. She really wasn't the enemy. "I mean it. It really is okay."

She smiled at me. "You're a good girl," she said. "You can't imagine how I worried about you, Amy, not knowing what you'd be like. Especially when I thought about Holly and Timmy, and what kind of influence you could have over them. But I can see your goodness. Mike's commented on it as well. You might not have been brought up with the same rules we go by, but there's a decency about you, an inherent goodness, that nothing, not even your father, could spoil."

Then again, maybe she was the enemy. I couldn't tell anymore. Someone had thrown away my scorecard. "I still don't think you should buy me anything too expensive," I said. I hated the idea of being trapped by bedroom furniture. "I'll be graduating next year and then I can get out of your hair."

"You're not in my hair!" my mother said, and she laughed. I didn't join her. "As a matter of fact, Mike and I were both hoping you'd go to college nearby and keep on living at home. There are a couple of excellent schools within commuting distance. Or if you need a year or so to adjust, you could go to the local community college. I've been hoping you'd give that furniture a lot of use."

"We don't have to decide that now," I said. "I just want you to know I can manage with a sofa bed for a while longer."

"Thank you, but it isn't necessary," my mother said. "I bet you had dreams of a bedroom, a really pretty one, your entire life. All girls do. Would you like us to change the wallpaper in your room? We went for something pretty neutral, but if you'd like flowers, or something like that, it's no bother."

"Oh, no, neutral is fine," I said. I couldn't remember what the wallpaper looked like, which was okay with me. "I'm not a flowery kind of a person."

"All right," she said. "I'm not either, not really. Holly likes them though, so I thought you might."

"Maybe you should go wallpaper shopping with Holly first," I said. "It really isn't fair that she has to wait."

"We're going on Friday," she said. "After school. I'm taking this whole week off, there's so much to do. And my parents are coming this weekend. You have no idea how excited they are, getting to see their granddaughter after so many years. My brother, Dick, and his wife and their kids are coming too. I bet you never knew you had cousins."

"No," I said.

"Your father's family is trash," she said. "He broke away from them when we got married, and he never made any effort to contact them after that. I'll give him credit for that. Of course he was in foster care a lot as a kid, so it wasn't like he ever really was close to any of them. But now you have grandparents and an aunt and uncle and cousins. All those people to love you, you never knew before."

Great. Fine. Just what I needed. "Where will they all stay?" I asked.

"Dick and Laura are just coming for the day," my mother replied. "My parents'll stay in your room, if you don't mind, and you and Holly can share for the night."

That should be a fun bonding experience, I thought. Dad had never talked much about his family. I'd gotten the feeling from him that families were something we were better off without. We had each other, and for a while we had Mona, and that was all we needed. Sure, I'd wanted a big family. I wanted to go to Disneyland, and I wanted a pony too. There'd even been a time I'd wanted a mommy.

Now I would have settled for Disneyland.

"This store is my favorite for furniture," my mother said, pulling into a parking lot. "But if there's nothing here you like, we can go someplace else."

"I'm sure they'll have lots of stuff," I said.

"How about a bed with a canopy?" my mother asked. "When you were little, I used to promise you a bed with a canopy for your eighth birthday." She was silent for a moment, and I once again regretted having to see her pain. "Or are you too old for that kind of thing now?"

"I don't know," I said. "I never really thought about a canopy."

"We'll see what they have," she said. "I don't want to dictate your choices. This is your bedroom, Amy. I want you to be happy with it for years to come."

"Thank you," I said.

We walked in, and my mother asked for directions to the bedroom sets. We trudged through a half mile of living rooms and dinettes before we saw what the store had to offer for sleeping.

"I love how many choices there are here," my mother whispered to me. Our saleswoman was hovering about, trying to decide which direction to point us in. French Provincial. Colonial. Art Deco. "Do you see anything that you like?"

The exit sign looked pretty good. "It's overwhelming," I said. "Could I just walk around a little?"

"Take your time," my mother said. "This is an important choice. I want you to be happy with it."

That was the problem. I really wished she wasn't so desperate for me to be happy, since that was the one thing I couldn't be for her.

I tried to concentrate on bedroom furniture. My room, my old room, hadn't been much to speak of. There was a bed, a chest of drawers, and a desk Dad had found at a yard sale once. I had a night table and a bookshelf and a chair from one of our old kitchens. Dad worked pretty steady, but he never had high-paying jobs, and he didn't believe in credit cards, so we only bought what we could afford. There were times when I resented that, when I saw my friends' bedrooms, and wished mine were like theirs, but I hadn't spent much time dreaming up a fantasy bedroom, any more than I'd spent time dreaming up a fantasy mother. Now I had both, and a headache the size of Ohio.

"They're all so pretty," my mother said. "And so different."

"Which one do you like the best?" I asked.

"It's not my choice," she said.

"I know that," I said. "But I could use the input."

She smiled at me. "I love this one," she admitted, leading me toward a set with a canopy bed. It was a pretty room.

"The furniture is made of cherry," the saleswoman said. "That's one of our prettiest rooms. Just perfect for a teenage girl."

"Amy's going to be sixteen in a couple of weeks," my mother said.

"It would be lovely for her," the saleswoman said. "I know my daughter would be thrilled having a room like this one."

"What do you think, Amy?" my mother asked. "Is it too frilly for you?"

"If it is, she doesn't have to keep the canopy on the bed all the time," the saleswoman said. "In the wintertime it makes things so cozy, but in the summer it can be re-moved for a more airy feeling."

My mother looked at me, her face so filled with hope, I wanted to pat her on her head. "It's so much money," I said. "I don't need anything this elaborate."

"You're a lucky woman," the saleswoman said. "My daughter would never say anything like that. The more it costs, the more she wants it."

"Amy isn't like that," my mother said. "Just the op-posite. But this time price is no object. We just want Amy to have the bedroom of her dreams."

"May I look a little longer?" I asked.

"As long as you want," the saleswoman said. "We have more bedrooms in this area as well."

I went in the direction she pointed. I had never seen so many beds, so many chests, so many brand-new pieces of furniture in my life.

When I was ten, Mona had bought my father a rocker recliner as a birthday present. We'd gone shopping for it together. I remembered sitting on all the different chairs, pretending to be Dad. Dad loved that chair; he still had it. Whenever we'd moved, that was the one thing he made sure to take with him. That and me.

What the hell was I going to do with a canopy bed? And why didn't Holly want one, so my mother would have her urge satisfied already?

"These rooms are nice too," my mother said. "But the better-quality things are in the first area."

"I wanted to save you the money," I said.

"Stop worrying about it," she said. She looked around to make sure the saleswoman wouldn't overhear. "This may be my fault," she said. "If you think we don't have enough money. When I said we didn't entertain much because of all the expense of looking for you. But honestly, Amy, we can afford a bedroom set for you. I know you haven't had much. I looked at your clothes last night, after you unpacked them. I want to buy you a whole new wardrobe. You deserve the best, and I've waited eleven years to have the chance to give it to you. It doesn't have to be the bed with the canopy. I'm not trying to dictate my tastes to you. But don't feel you have to settle for cheap. Don't do that to me."

That's what it came down to. Doing for her. I was deluding myself if I thought I could get away with something impersonal, something guest-roomish, something nobody would expect me to think of as mine. "I'd love the canopy set," I said. "It's beautiful."

"Are you sure?" my mother asked. "You're not saying that just to please me?"

Of course I was. "Of course not," I said. "I guess taste does run in the family. I just never thought I could ever own anything that pretty."

She hugged me. "You're going to own the best from now on," she said. "It's what you deserve."

The saleswoman seemed pleased by my decision as well. My mother whipped out a charge card and discussed delivery dates. The furniture would come next Tuesday. Could I wait that long?

"No problem," I said.

"We should get curtains to match the canopy," my mother said. "Do you want to do that today, or would you prefer going clothes shopping now?"

"I really don't need any new clothes," I said. "And the curtains in the room are fine." I could just picture myself at the Freak-of-the-Month Club meeting explaining my life was a living hell because all my mother wanted to do was buy me things.

"I'll tell you what," my mother said. "Why don't we stop in at Talbott's on the way home? It's a wonderful department store, the old-fashioned kind that has everything, and maybe you'll see something that excites you. A new dress for you to wear on Saturday. Or sheets or a bedspread. Something that'll feel like a present."

"I don't need any presents," I said, but I could feel my resolve weakening. What was wrong with being given a few things, especially if it was going to make her so happy? She had eleven years of shopping fantasies stored away inside her, and who was I to deprive her of one day of madness?

"All girls need new clothes," my mother said. "Come on, Amy. Let's buy you something wonderful."

And we did. As a matter of fact, we bought out half of Talbott's. We bought two dresses, three skirts, two blouses, a pair of slacks, three pairs of shoes, a jacket, a blazer, two lightweight sweaters, socks, underwear, two sets of sheets, a bedspread, a combination clock radio–cassette player, and three cassettes to play on it. I didn't know if she was going to be able to buy my love, but I had to give her credit for trying.

"What is all this?" Mike asked when we got home. "Did you leave anything in the stores?"

"Not very much," my mother said. She looked younger than before, and happier, and I could see that Mike had noticed it as well. He helped us unload the car and then carried some of the bags to my bedroom for me.

"Did you have fun?" he asked me as I plopped things down.

I nodded. "She's so nice," I said. "And it was her idea to buy most of this stuff. Honest."

He laughed. "I know," he said. "I recognize her style. Thank you for indulging her. It meant a lot."

"It's okay," I said. "I'm sorry about the eleven years. I really am. I wish I could have done things differently."

"You were a kid," Mike said. "You're not responsible for any of it. And I appreciate the effort you're making now. I know this is hard on you, all these changes. It can't be easy, walking into so much love. I've very grateful to you, for not whining and weeping and setting things on fire."

I laughed. "I hadn't thought of it," I said. "Thanks for the suggestion."

"Do it before the new furniture arrives, okay?" he said. "Do you need hangers for all these new dresses?"

I checked the closet. "There are plenty here," I said. "Thanks anyway."

"Then I'll go finish supper," he said. "We'll be eating in about fifteen minutes."

"I'll be there," I said. I liked Mike. He was easier than my mother. I wondered what it would have been like having him as a stepfather all those years, whether I would have liked him as much. He really did seem like a nice guy.

I sat down on the sofa bed and felt a lurch of guilt and nausea. No matter how nice Mike seemed, he wasn't my father. Sure it was dazzling to buy all those things. We'd spent more on clothes today than I had in three years. I'm human. I love owning things.

But love isn't about presents. It's about being there, and caring, and whether it was fair to my mother or not, she hadn't been there, and my father had. Mike could be the nicest guy in the world, but he still wasn't my father. He hadn't made sure I'd done my homework or practiced the tuba or memorized my lines in the school play.

I'd felt this way before once. It was right after Dad and Mona had gotten married. I'd been so glad when they had, so happy to have a mother again. Mona was the kind of person you always knew where you stood with, and as far as she was concerned, I was her daughter, and she loved me heart and soul. No matter how great Dad was, I needed that kind of love, and I sucked it into me and felt like the luckiest kid in America.

One day Dad and I had a fight, I don't even remember about what, and I shouted at him, "I don't love you anymore. I love Mona more than I love you."

He'd been in a rage until I said that, but as soon as the words came out, his expression changed. He didn't even look sad, just lost. I couldn't bear to see him look that way, and I ran out of the room into my bedroom.

Mona was out when we had the fight, and she came

into my room a little later. "Your father told me what you said, Brooke," she said.

"I meant it," I said, resentful that Dad had told her. "I do too love you more."

"No, you don't," she said. "And you may not know it, but that's about the cruelest thing you could have said to your father."

I never meant to be cruel. Cruelty was something Daddy really hated, even more than not living up to your responsibilities. "Why was it cruel?" I asked. "Isn't it okay for me to love you?"

"It's fine," she said. "And I love you too, and that's fine. But he's your father. He's the one who raised you and loved you and took care of you."

"I know," I said. "But he won't let me sleep over at Katie's." That's what the fight had been about. I wanted to spend the weekend at Katie's, and Dad wouldn't let me. God, the things you hurt people over. It's a wonder any marriages survive.

"Your father has his reasons," Mona said. "He doesn't think Katie's parents are reliable. You know he said Katie could come here instead."

"But she's having a sleepover," I said. "All the other girls are going."

"Maybe their fathers don't worry as much as yours does," Mona said. "Maybe their fathers don't care as much either."

"I didn't mean to be cruel," I said. "Is Daddy mad at me?"

"He's hurt," Mona said. "You know, when he was a

boy, nobody much loved him. That does funny things to you. Sometimes it makes you feel like nobody ever will love you, like you don't deserve to be loved. Can you understand that?"

I shook my head.

Mona smiled at me. "That's because you've grown up loved," she said. "If your father hadn't been there for you when your mother died, I think you'd understand only too well."

Dammit. Another stroll down memory lane leading straight to a lie. My mother hadn't died. She'd just been out shopping.

"Amy! Dinner's ready!"

I looked at all the unpacked shopping bags, all the bright and shiny new things Amy Donovan had been given that afternoon. Brooke Eastman didn't exist anymore. She never really had. She'd just been a fantasy, Dad's fantasy motherless daughter. As real as that trip to Disneyland.

"Coming!" I said. Bye-bye, Brooke. Welcome, Amy.

8

The phone rang near lunchtime on Saturday. Holly answered it. "Hello?" she said. "Oh. Wait a second. Amy, it's for you."

In the five days I'd spent being Amy Donovan, this was the first phone call I'd gotten. Wildly, irrationally, I thought it was Dad, and I raced to take the call.

"Hi, Amy? This is Chris Quinn. From Teens in Crisis."

"Oh, sure, hi," I said. I knew it couldn't be Dad. He wasn't allowed to call. It was scary how much I'd wanted it to be him though.

"I'm just calling because you didn't come on Friday," he said. "I wanted to make sure you knew where we met."

"The Unitarian Church," I said. "I remembered. I just, well, I didn't feel like I needed to go."

"That's fine," Chris said. "You're under no obligation. We just wanted you to know you're welcome anytime. Okay?"

"Thanks," I said. "I appreciate that."

"Okay," he said. "Well, I'd better get off now. I'll see you Monday, at school."

"Thanks again," I said, hanging up the phone.

"Is that your boyfriend?" Holly asked.

"No, it's just a guy I know," I said.

"I bet it's your boyfriend," Holly said. "I bet you're lying."

"You lose the bet," I said.

"Mom, Amy got a call from a boy," Holly called.

"That's nice," my mother said. "Holly, come set the table. We want everything to be perfect for this afternoon."

Holly gave me a dirty look, and I shot one right back at her. Tim wasn't too bad, especially when I compared him with Charleen's kids, but Holly was a pain and a half. When I thought about her rationally, I could sympathize with her situation. But mostly I wanted to kill her.

"Today's a big day," Mike said to me as I fantasized strangling his daughter. "You ready for some new relatives, Amy?"

"As ready as I'll ever be," I said. "I never had grandparents before. It'll be fun having some."

"I was very close to my grandparents," Mike said. "I always felt sorry for kids who weren't."

"And an aunt and uncle," I said. "And two cousins. Danny and Steffi." I'd been rehearsing their names all week.

"Do you remember any of them?" Mike asked. "You used to stay at your grandparents' a lot when you were little."

"I don't think so," I said.

"It isn't surprising," Mike said. "Little kids remember things when they talk about them with their parents. Holly remembers the cat we used to have, because she and I would talk about him after he died. Your father didn't let you talk about things like that, so your memories all died out."

As statements about my father went, that one was fairly neutral. It was also true. I resented it anyway. "What should I call them?" I asked. "My grandparents."

"The kids call them Granny and Gramps," Mike said. "Do you think you could manage that?"

Granny and Gramps. They sounded so American. "I can try," I said.

"Your grandmother told me last year she never thought she'd live to see you again," Mike said. "I don't think you can imagine how much this means to them, having you back."

"It means a lot to me too," I said. "I'd better go upstairs now, make sure the room is ready for them."

"Okay," Mike said. "And don't worry if you feel a little shy. I was nervous the first time I met your mother's family also."

I smiled at him and went upstairs. Mike had gotten me through that week. I was glad my mother had married him. As weird as everything had been for me, things would have been a whole lot weirder without him around.

I was still upstairs when the doorbell rang. Holly ran to get it. I allowed her a couple of minutes without me for hugs and kisses, but before I went downstairs, the door-bell rang a second time, and the rest of the family arrived.

There was no avoiding it. I had to go down there and meet everyone. I knew I should be glad about it. I'd dreamed about aunts and uncles, cousins and grandpar-ents, when I was younger. I even remembered feeling hurt that they hadn't wanted to see me, back in the days when I thought my mother was dead. Had I confronted Dad about that? I had vague memories of his telling me they were too busy taking care of the new baby, but I wasn't sure if that really happened, or if I'd just made it up. I used to be able to remember everything. Now half the time I couldn't remember my own name, either of them.

"Amy, come on down!" my mother shouted. "There are people here who want to say hello."

So I got to make the grand entrance. I was certainly dressed for the occasion, in one of my new dresses and new pairs of shoes.

"Oh, she's beautiful," my grandmother said.

"She looks just like Hal," my grandfather said.

"She doesn't look anything like him," my grand-mother said. "Betty, she's the spitting image of you as a teenager."

"You're crazy," my grandfather said. "Betty was much prettier."

"Dad, shut up," my uncle, Dick, said. "Amy, don't pay any attention to him. Come on down, so we can hug you."

I felt like a total idiot walking down those stairs. I

should have been waiting with the others, I told myself, not acting like some big-shot movie star. And I did look like my father, I always had and I always will, and no matter what kind of dresses my mother bought for me, no one looking at the two of us would automatically assume we were mother and daughter. For the first time in almost a week I had one of those maybe-this-is-all-a-mistake feelings. I didn't look like any of these new blood relatives of mine. Maybe the real Amy Michelle Donovan was still running around loose, trying desperately to convince *Still Missing* that they'd gotten the wrong girl.

"Give me a kiss, darling," my grandmother said. I walked over and hugged her. She looked like my mother, and she didn't look especially Grannyish either. She and my grandfather were both younger-looking than I'd expected.

After I finished hugging her, I hugged my grandfather, who seemed about as excited by it as I was. Next came Uncle Dick and then Aunt Laura. Nobody seemed to expect me to hug Danny or Steffi, so we just stared at each other for a moment.

"Lunch is ready," my mother said. "Holly and Timmy have been helping me all morning."

"Do you cook, Amy?" Aunt Laura asked.

"A little," I said.

"Your mother's a wonderful cook," Uncle Dick said. "She takes after Mom that way. Doesn't she, Dad?"

"They're both good cooks," Gramps said.

"Do Danny and Steffi cook?" I asked. Danny was

fourteen, and Steffi eleven, so there was no reason why they couldn't cook.

"They're whizzes with the microwave," Aunt Laura said. "Tell us, Amy, what's this week been like for you? I imagine it's been just thrilling."

Thrilling. A whole new word to add to my vocabulary. "It's been very exciting," I said. "And this is real exciting too, meeting all of you. I mean, meeting you again."

"Don't you remember any of us at all?" Granny asked. "All those years away from us, didn't you think about us ever?"

"Don't forget, Mom, Hal fed her a bunch of lies," Uncle Dick said. "What exactly did he tell you about us, Amy?"

"Come on, let's all sit down for lunch," my mother said. "Dad, Mom, sit over here by Amy. Kids, why don't you sit together. Mike, would you lead us in grace?"

This grace business was something I still hadn't gotten used to. Before supper every day Mike said grace. He didn't always say the same thing either.

Dad and I had never gone to church, not even at Christmas. "Religion's fine if you like that sort of thing," Dad had told me, when I'd asked if I could go to church with some friend of mine or another. "I'll never stop you. But I'll never go with you either." I hadn't gone. He and Mona had been married by a justice of the peace, and I couldn't remember Mona going to church either. If my grandparents went to church tomorrow with everyone else, there'd be no way of my avoiding it. I hoped I could figure out when to stand up and when to sit down.

"Dear God, we thank You for Your many wonderful blessings," Mike said. We had all bowed our heads. I'd figured that trick out almost immediately. "And we especially thank You today for this family reunion, one we have all prayed for and that we can now enjoy. Our hearts are filled with gratitude for this and everything else You have bestowed upon us. May we prove worthy of Your great love. Amen."

"Amen," we all said.

"I was asking Amy about what Hal used to say about us," Uncle Dick declared. "What kind of lies he fed her."

Everyone looked at me. I wished we were back saying grace.

"I'm not sure Amy remembers," Mike said.

"How can she not remember?" Uncle Dick asked. "She remembered Betty well enough to call that eight-hundred number. And she hadn't seen her since she was five."

"That was a fluke," I said. "I didn't really recognize her anyway. It was Dad I recognized."

I knew immediately from the quality of the silence that I'd just said a big wrong thing.

"You didn't remember Mommy?" Holly asked.

"I don't think Amy meant it quite that way," Mike said.

"How did she mean it, then?" Gramps asked. "It sure sounded like she didn't remember her own mother, the way she said it."

"What does it matter?" my mother asked. "Mom, help yourself to some chicken. It's that new recipe I told you about, low-fat fried."

"How could a girl not remember her own mother?" Granny asked. "Amy, darling, you must have recognized your mother. Seeing her picture on TV must have jarred all kinds of memories."

"I was seven when my father died," Gramps said. "And I'll remember what he looked like to the day I die."

Uncle Dick shook his head. "The lies that man must have told you," he said. "You know, I never liked Hal. I never trusted him. I tried to talk you out of marrying him, Betty. Remember? I knew it would be a mistake."

"I don't think Betty would have married him if circumstances had been different," Granny said.

Circumstances? This was the first I'd heard about circumstances.

"I don't think any of this is appropriate dinner-table conversation," Mike said. "Laura, how's your new job going?"

"I really like it," she said.

"Is it much of an adjustment for the kids?" Mike asked. "They're not used to your working."

"They're doing fine," Laura said. "Aren't you, kids?"

"What's a 'circumstance'?" Steffi asked.

"All Granny meant was if things had been different, Aunt Betty wouldn't have married Hal," Laura said.

"Different how?" Danny asked.

"Mommy, my stomach hurts," Tim said. His stomach had been hurting almost constantly since I'd moved in.

"Don't eat if you don't want to," my mother said.

"My stomach hurts too," Holly said.

"It does not," my mother said. "Holly, behave yourself and eat your lunch."

"How come Timmy doesn't have to eat and I do?" Holly asked.

"Because Timmy's younger than you are," my mother said.

"Really, Holly, this chicken is delicious," Laura said. "Isn't it, kids?"

"Yeah, it's great," Danny said. He was the only one at the table eating. "Could you pass the coleslaw?"

I passed it.

"Great," he said.

"Danny would eat on the *Titanic*," Uncle Dick said.

"He's a growing boy," Granny said. "Growing boys need their nourishment. When I think how much you used to eat at his age, it's a wonder we could afford to clothe you."

"Isn't Amy's dress pretty?" my mother asked. "We bought it together on Tuesday. Amy and I had quite a shopping spree Tuesday."

"You told me on the phone," Aunt Laura said. "It sounded like so much fun."

"It's been wonderful having Amy home again," my mother said. "A dream come true."

The only circumstance I could think of that would guarantee marriage was if my mother had been pregnant with me. And if that was true, I resented my born-again-virgin status.

"Do you like your new school, Amy?" Aunt Laura asked. "It can be so hard changing schools, especially midyear."

"It's fine," I said. "Everyone's been very nice." That speech I could say in my sleep.

"We've been tremendously impressed with the adjustment Amy's made," Mike said. "She's fit right into the family."

"And why shouldn't she?" Granny asked. "This is her family. It's where she's belonged all these years."

"Yeah, but God only knows what Hal did to her," Uncle Dick said. "I wouldn't trust him with a dog, let alone a daughter."

"Amy's father is the worst man that ever lived," Holly said.

"I don't know if he's the worst," Uncle Dick said. "But he's on my top-ten list."

"Now, Dick," Aunt Laura said.

"I'm sorry, Laura, but I know what Betty went through," Uncle Dick said. "And I'm not about to forget it. He put her through hell when they were married, and then he put her through worse when he snatched Amy. She suffered eleven years, more, from that man. I've never known anybody who caused more pain, and that includes your brother, Martin."

"I thought we weren't going to discuss Martin," Aunt Laura said.

"We're not," Uncle Dick said. "I'm just using him as

a comparison point, so you'll see how bad Hal Donovan is."

"We don't discuss Hal," Mike said. "Not in front of the kids."

"That's not true, Daddy," Holly said. "You used to discuss him all the time, how mean he was and how much he hurt Mommy."

"In the past we did," Mike said. "But not anymore."

"But why not?" Holly asked. "He didn't stop being mean."

"That is such a pretty dress," Granny said. "It goes so well with your coloring, Amy. Betty, you should wear blue more often."

"I've never liked blue on me," my mother said. "It's a great color on Holly though."

"Amy and Holly don't look anything alike," Gramps said. "You'd never know they were sisters, to look at them."

"They're half sisters, Gramps," Danny said. "Half sisters don't always look alike. Could you please pass the biscuits?"

"I'm glad I don't look like Amy," Holly said.

Danny laughed. "You couldn't look like her," he said. "She looks like her father, and you have a different father."

"And a much nicer one," Aunt Laura said.

"No comparison," Gramps said. "Hal Donovan was a bum. I could never figure out what Betty saw in him in the first place."

"I made a mistake," my mother said. "Do you mind?

I thought there was something in him, something good, worth having, and I was wrong. You all were right, and I was wrong. I know I'm the only person at this table who ever made a mistake, so I'm very sorry. Now, can we please change the subject?"

"So, Amy, I bet you're looking forward to seeing yourself on TV tonight," Uncle Dick said. "I bet it was a kick for Holly and Timmy to see themselves last week."

"We're going to be on again tonight too," Holly said. "They interviewed all of us when Amy came home."

"I wish I was on TV," Steffi said. "I wanted to come on Tuesday so I could have been on TV too, but Mom wouldn't let me."

"I told you it would be too crowded if we all showed up," Aunt Laura said.

"It was real crowded anyway," Holly said. "Everybody on the block was here. It was like a big party."

"See, Mom, I could've come," Steffi said. "Now I'll never be on TV."

"I'm sorry," Aunt Laura said. "At the time it seemed best for us to stay home."

"It must have been pretty overwhelming for you, Amy," Uncle Dick said. "But I bet you were excited when you saw what a nice house your mother had."

"This house cost too damn much money," Gramps said. "They mortgaged their entire future when they bought it."

"Did you live in a house, Amy?" Aunt Laura asked.

Uncle Dick laughed. "How could Hal Donovan ever afford a house?" he asked. "He had to borrow fifty bucks from me when Amy was born. Never paid me back either, if I remember correctly."

"We lived in an apartment," I said.

"More like a slum, I'll bet," Uncle Dick said.

"Can I go outside and play?" Tim asked.

"Sure," Mike said. "Danny, are you finished eating? Would you mind going out with Timmy?"

"Okay," Danny said, his mouth stuffed with chicken. "Come on, Timmy. Let's play some ball."

"Can Steffi and I watch TV?" Holly asked.

"Just for a little while," her mother said. "Your grandparents want to see both of you."

"Come on, Steffi," Holly said. The two girls ran out of the dining room.

"This is better," Uncle Dick said. "Now we can really get to meet Amy. We can talk honestly, without worrying about what the kids might think."

"No third degrees," Mike said.

"I just keep wondering what that son of a bitch said about us," Uncle Dick said. "All those years he kept Amy from us."

"I'd like to know too," Gramps said. "I'd like to know what kind of lies he fed my granddaughter."

I don't know if I would have answered except I could feel my mother looking at me as well. She'd been good about not asking me things, better than I would have been, I suspected, but now her brother and her father were here, and she didn't have to pretend not to care anymore. I didn't know if I owed her the truth, I was no longer sure who I owed what to, but I knew I couldn't lie, and I doubted I could use an aching stomach as an excuse.

"He told me she was dead," I said. "When I first started living with him. And then later on I found out she wasn't, and he said she didn't want me."

"And you believed him?" my grandmother asked. "You actually believed a mother wouldn't want her own daughter?"

Had I believed that? Hadn't I had some doubts? I was eleven years old when Dad had admitted my mother was still alive. "He said he had contacted her, and she had told him to keep me," I said. Maybe he was a son of a bitch. Maybe he did belong on the top-ten list.

Uncle Dick shook his head. "What a bum," he said. "Betty, I'm sorry you ever met that man."

"He really told you that?" my mother asked. "That I said I didn't want you?"

I nodded.

"I never," she said. "I never heard from him. We hired detectives, we went to every agency in America that dealt with missing children, we put posters up, we ran want ads, we did everything we could think of to try to find you. God only knows what it did to Holly and Timmy, our looking for you. The only reason my marriage survived is because Mike's a saint. I used to dream, night after night, that the doorbell was ringing and you were there. We used to pray for your safety when we said grace. I bought you presents every year on your birthday, and Christmas, Christmas was a shambles for years because I was in so much pain. And he told you I said I didn't want you?"

"I'm sorry," I said.

"And you still love him," she said. "You do, I know it, and I bet you'd still like to be with him, in spite of what he did to me."

"Betty, stop it," Mike said. "We know this is going to take time. This is harder on Amy than on any of us."

"No, it's okay," I said. "I'll stop loving him. I will. I promise. I already love you, because you've been so nice, and I bet one day real soon I won't love him anymore."

"We're not asking that of you," Mike said, but we all knew they were, that my mother was, that that was the price I was expected to pay for eleven years of willingly believing in lies. It wasn't that big a price either, I told myself, as I looked at my mother, who was trying so hard not to cry, my mother and her parents and brother, my blood kin who had been kept strangers from me. Not a big price at all to love someone who loved you and to stop loving someone who ultimately loved only himself. One day soon I was sure to feel the right way. One day she'd be Mom, and I'd be Amy, and Dad would be nothing at all.

9

I'd spent Monday trying to love my mother, but by Tuesday I was already crazed by the need to talk to someone who really knew and loved me. Dad was out of the question, but Mona was worth the risk. So after school I dawdled for as long a time as I could, and then, when I was reasonably sure Mona would be home from work but Mike and my mother wouldn't be, I started pouring my change into the pay phone. I'd learned my lesson that last week and kept every nickel, dime, and quarter that came my way.

I was in luck. Mona was home and answered on the first ring. It made me feel she was sitting there, waiting for me to call, and for the first time in over a week I felt that rush of love that comes only with security.

"Mona, it's me," I said.

"Brooke?" she said.

Just hearing my name was music. "I needed to hear your voice," I said. "How are you?"

"I'm fine," she said. "Worried about you, of course,

but fine. How are you? Is everything okay? Are they treating you okay?"

"They're really trying," I said. "But I miss you and Dad and home so much. Have you spoken to him? Is he all right?"

"He's hanging in there," Mona said. "We spoke a couple of times this weekend."

"I met my family this weekend," I said. "My grandparents, I mean, and my aunt and uncle and cousins."

"That's wonderful," Mona said. Clearly she had never met them. "Grandparents. I loved my grandmother. That's a very special relationship."

"I suppose," I said.

"Give it time," Mona said. "How's your mother? This must be difficult for her too."

It honestly hadn't occurred to me that it was. "I don't know," I said. "She seems real happy. Happy and excited."

"I'm glad," Mona said. "She's very lucky to have you as a daughter."

"Mona, I don't want to be here," I said. "I want to go home."

"No, Brooke," Mona said. "I mean, I know that's how you feel, but it's wrong. The judge was right when he told you to go with your mother. Even those rules he set up, no matter how much you might hate them, they were right too."

"Eighty-five cents, please, for the next two minutes," the operator said.

"Wait a second," I said, searching for the right

change. I located the needed quarters and dime and slid them in.

"This is a wonderful opportunity for you," Mona said when we were sanctioned again by the phone company. "You're finally going to have a family. A real one. That's something your father and I never had for you. Grandparents. Cousins. Brothers and sisters. So many people who love you. People you can love."

"I know," I said. "But it's overwhelming."

"That's why the judge gave you all that time," Mona said. "He knew it couldn't just happen. But, Brooke, honey, it's not even just love. They have money too. Maybe not a fortune, but compared with your dad, even your dad and me when we were pooling our salaries, it's an awful lot. Admit it. Don't you have a nicer room there than you used to?"

"I don't care about the money," I said. "I'd rather be home."

"Maybe you don't care now because you're so mad at the world," Mona replied. "But that won't last, and the things money can buy will. I'm not saying you should let them buy your love. You're not that kind of person. It wouldn't happen. But they're going to love you anyway, and they can give you clothes and an education and a pretty bedroom in a real house. Your dad and I always wanted you to have those things, but we could never afford them."

"I don't need them," I said. "I got along fine without a house."

"You'll get along even better with one," Mona said.

"Never underrate money, Brooke. That's a damn-fool mistake."

"But I don't love her," I said. It was funny how good that felt, to say those words out loud. "I don't know her and I don't love her."

"Give yourself half a chance, and you will," Mona said. "She's your mother, Brooke. She carried you for nine months and gave birth to you. That's a bond that never goes away."

"You love me like a mother," I said. "Even without that."

"I love you like a mother," Mona said. "You're right. And I couldn't love you more if you were my own flesh and blood. But, Brooke, don't kid yourself. You can use all the love you can get. Your dad is a great guy, but he isn't exactly one hundred percent perfect. Neither am I, if you get right down to it."

"Neither is she," I said.

"Give her a chance," Mona said. "And, honey, I don't think you should call me anymore."

"Eighty-five cents for the next two minutes."

This time it was harder finding the right combination of change. I put in all the dimes I could find and hoped they added up to enough.

"Fifteen cents more, please."

"Mona, don't go," I said. I rifled through my pocket and located a quarter. The phone company got a dime's donation from me. I hoped they'd use it for worthy causes. "Mona, what do you mean, I shouldn't call you?"

"It isn't right," Mona said. "It's like cheating. Like

you're not being faithful. They're your family now, not your dad and me, and the judge knew what he was doing, and you should respect that. You're never going to love your mother if you think, 'Well, I can always love Mona instead.' So don't think it. I may love you like a mother, but now you have a real, honest-to-goodness mother to love you instead."

"Don't you love me anymore?" I asked.

"Don't give me that crap," Mona said. "I'll love you to the day I die, and you know that. But that still doesn't make me your mother. Your father did something so bad to you, honey. Not just to you either. That's what broke us up, me learning what he'd done. It meant I could never have kids if I stayed with him. You stay with your mother. You let her show you how much she loves you, and you take your time, but learn to love her back. And get down on your knees some night and thank God that you have grandparents and aunts and uncles and brothers and sisters to love. You've gotten the best damn break a kid could ever get, and you learn to be grateful for it, and then, when you can honestly say, 'This is my family and I love them,' then you can call me and we'll take it from there."

"Mona," I said, but she'd already hung up. I clicked the receiver a couple of times to see if that would magically retrieve her, but she was gone. I told myself not to be surprised. Mona had left me before. When she and Dad divorced, she moved out on us. Sure, we stayed in touch. I saw her a lot, and Dad saw her sometimes himself, although they both acted like that didn't count for anything. But for three years, one before she married Dad and two after, she'd lived with us, and been as close to a mom as I'd ever had, and then one day, after a lot of crying and carrying on, she was out of there, and Dad and I were back to being alone. Dad said we didn't need her, and he'd been right. We got along just fine, maybe even better, because it hurt when she and Dad fought, and that was pretty much all the time toward the end. So she was gone again. So what was the big deal? If I could get along without her when I didn't have a mother, I was bound to do great now that I really did have one.

I beat Mike and my mother home and went straight to my pretty bedroom in my pretty house and did all my pretty homework. When I finished that, I opened up my closet and looked at all my pretty new clothes and then checked out my brand-new chest of drawers and looked at all the pretty clothes in there. I found the picture I'd brought of Dad and Mona and me, and I almost tore it up, but instead I hid it facedown under a pile of pretty new sweaters. There were six pretty new sweaters in that drawer. Last year for Christmas I'd gotten one from Mona, and that had been it. Six new sweaters, and there were months to go before it was Christmas again.

I knew six sweaters to one didn't mean my mother loved me six times more than Mona did, but I suspected there was some kind of algebraic formula, with love being X and money being Y, that would equal out to six if I could just work it out. Dad had bought me a typewriter for Christmas, and Mike and Uncle Dick had discussed what kind of computer I should have. The formula had to shift there. Dad was bound to love me more than Mike did.

It's funny how the most obvious thoughts slap you in the face sometimes. If Dad was bound to love me more than Mike did, then my mother was bound to love me more than Mona. It was algebra again, some magical combination of symbols that added up to flesh and blood. I didn't know the formula yet, but once I worked it out, then everything would be okay. I'd know just who to love and how much. I wouldn't be poor little Brooke without a mother anymore. I'd be lucky Amy with moms and dads and brothers and sisters and typewriters and computers and everything else that came with two identities.

So I hardly even minded when my mother knocked on my door and didn't wait for me to tell her to come in before she did. She was my mother, after all, the Big X, and she knew she was welcome even before I did.

"Mike's making supper," she said. "I just got home from work, and I thought I'd see how you're doing."

"Great," I said. "I finished my homework already."

"How's school?" she asked. "Are you making friends?"

"I think so," I said. "I mean, I am, but I haven't been there very long yet, you know, so I'm not really close to anybody yet."

"You probably miss your old friends," my mother said. "Mike and I talked about that, what we should do. If you want to write to them, you certainly can, but we don't think it's a good idea for them to visit you."

"Oh, no," I said. "Besides, they're too far away. No,

I don't mind making new friends. We used to move around a lot. I'm used to going to new schools."

My mother reached out and brushed my hair with her hand. I hardly even flinched. "You've had it rough," she said. "Rougher than I realize, I think."

I didn't argue.

"There are so many reasons I wish we could have found you sooner," my mother said. "All the obvious ones of course. But I wish you'd had more of a chance to grow up here, in this house, in this town. This is your home, Amy, and a girl's entitled to a real home, a place she always knows is hers. That's a gift we've been able to give to Holly and Timmy, but not you. Not until now."

"It's nice," I said, not knowing what the hell I meant by that. If my mother didn't understand either, she didn't ask for a translation.

"Do you like your new school?" she asked instead. "It must be very different from your old one."

"It's cleaner," I said. "And the classes are smaller."

"We moved to this town for its school district," my mother said. "Mike and I both think education is terribly important. He made me go back to school after Timmy was born. I was still so crazed about you, I could barely do anything except worry over my babies, and Mike insisted I go back. I'd had a little bit of college before I married Hal, but of course once we were married, there was no talk about my being in school. There was no money. It was a struggle finding enough for the rent every month. But Mike insisted, and he was right. Just being in school grounded me. I became a better mother and a much better wife, and I lucked out with a terrific job when I graduated. It's funny. I was raising the kids and working part-time and going to school, and even with all that I felt stronger than I had since Hal kidnapped you. More optimistic too. My faith in God grew stronger, and I knew He wouldn't make me go through life without ever seeing you again. Mike used to say that too, that God would know when the moment would be right for you to come back to me. And He did. I know it was God that made you watch that TV show that night and call the number. The moment was right."

I wondered if maybe she had a point. Under ordinary circumstances I would have been out that night, eating pizza with all my friends, throwing myself at Jason Best. And no one would have recognized me from that computer picture. I didn't myself. Dad had always felt that God was fine for other people, so I didn't have much of an acquaintance with how He operated. Mike and my mother obviously did, in which case the moment was right, and some great cosmic injustice had been corrected, and Charleen wouldn't even be billed for it.

"I really appreciate all you've been doing for me," I said. "It must be kind of weird for you, having this grown-up kid in your house. You can't be used to it."

"It isn't weird," my mother said. "It's wonderful. No, it's amazing. I think 'Amy's back,' and it's the most wonderful feeling, like the rabbit's been pulled out of the hat, or the one scarf turns into a hundred. I don't know. It's like a rose that you find after the first snowfall. Does that make any sense to you?" She laughed, and I noticed how pretty she was when she laughed. It was a good laugh too, warm and loving.

I wanted to give her something in return for that laugh, something other than feigned concern and gratitude. I searched for just the right thing to say, but when you have to search, the laughter dies, and then there's only silence.

"I should see what's going on downstairs," my mother said, and I knew she didn't realize my silence wasn't rejection but a failed effort at love.

"No," I said. "Stay here, just a little longer. Okay?"

"Of course it's okay." I could tell from her smile how little it took for me to please her. *She's happy with crumbs*, I thought. *Even I must have some crumbs for her.*

"There's so much I don't know," I said. It was the first rule of getting a boy interested in you. Ask him questions. If it worked for boys, it should work for mothers. "Like how did you and Mike meet?"

"We met at the zoo," my mother said. "Isn't that funny? I had you with me, and he was alone. He'd just moved to the area, and he'd heard there was a really good zoo, and he decided to check it out. We met in front of the giraffes. We've given each other giraffes ever since, you know, ceramic ones or stuffed animals."

"That's nice," I said. "It's kind of romantic."

"We think so," my mother said. "And when the kids are acting up and one of us complains it's a zoo, we both laugh, and that always makes things better."

"And your parents," I said. "I mean Granny and Gramps. How did they meet?"

"At church," my mother said. "But you ought to ask them about that. They'd be thrilled to answer your questions."

"I'll do that," I said, trying to come up with another question for her. But everything I thought of was either too personal or not personal enough. They ought to provide you with a list, Questions for Your Mother, when they throw you into the loving arms of one. Next time I saw the judge, I'd be sure to tell him that.

"You and Dick," I said. "Uncle Dick. Did the two of you always get along, or was it a zoo sometimes when you were kids?"

"All brothers and sisters fight sometimes," my mother said. "You'll learn that soon enough. But Dick and I were always close. He's always been very protective of me. And he's never been shy about letting me know when I was making a big mistake."

Like marrying Dad, I thought, and I knew she was thinking it too, so we both moved on to safer turf. "That must be nice," I said. "Having a big brother to protect you."

"It's the one thing I've never been able to give any of my children," my mother said. "But now at least Holly has her big sister back. That's going to be a very special relationship for her, having you to look up to and confide in."

Yeah. Right. I hoped we weren't supposed to hold our breath until that one happened.

"When you were away," my mother said. "All those years. Did you have someone you could confide in?"

"Sure," I said. "Mona." I was so surprised by the question, it hardly even hurt to say her name.

"Mona," my mother said. "Hal's lady friend."

"His wife," I said. "I mean his ex-wife."

"They were married?" my mother said. "I didn't realize."

"For two years," I said.

My mother looked at me.

"They were," I said. "I was at the wedding. I saw the divorce papers. It was all legal. They were as married—"
As you and Mike are, I almost said, but stopped myself.

"Two years," my mother said instead. "Two years out of eleven."

"Well, they were together before then too," I said. "And afterward we always stayed in touch. I used to spend weekends with her, and I talked to her a lot on the phone. She was great to me." I couldn't believe I was defending her, when she'd dumped me two hours earlier.

"I'm sure she's very nice," my mother said, and she used *nice* just the way I did, to mean a thousand things, none of which was necessarily pleasant. "Why did she and Hal split up? Do you happen to know?"

"They were fighting," I said.

"About what?" my mother asked.

"Things," I said. "It was a long time ago. I was just a kid."

"Did they fight about the way Hal was treating you?" my mother asked. "Did Mona disapprove of how he was raising you?"

"He raised me fine," I said, and I could hear my voice getting shrill. "That wasn't what they fought about."

"Then, what was it?" my mother asked. "I'm not being nosy, Amy. I have a right to know what Hal put you through, all those years away from me."

"He didn't put me through anything," I said. "Not the way you mean. And he and Mona fought over all the usual stuff. Whose friends were nicer. What to watch on TV that night."

"Nobody divorces over television," my mother said. "There had to have been more to it than that."

"I don't remember," I said.

"There's a lot you don't seem to remember," my mother said, and the woman who had laughed was gone and had been replaced by Mrs. Girard. "I'm sure that's Hal's fault. Making you move around, changing everything, even your age. Lie after lie after lie. It's a wonder you can remember your own name."

Which of course I couldn't. "I think I hear Mike calling you," I said.

She looked at me, and then she turned back into my mother and wasn't just Mrs. Girard anymore. "I'll go see," she said, and she bent over and kissed me before getting up.

I watched as she left my room and I thought about her laugh and wondered how many times she'd been able to laugh over the past eleven years. Mona was right. I owed her the chance to love me. And if I didn't have

Mona anymore, I was a fool to throw away the only mother I did have.

It'll work out, I told myself. *Someday all the Xs and Ys will make sense to me, and I'll know how to love my mother and be part of a family, and the winter rose will bloom for me.*

10

The letter was waiting for me when I got home from school on Thursday. School was getting easier. I had experience with new schools and not knowing anyone, but I hadn't been able to shake that feeling of longing and disbelief at the Girards. And she was still "my mother"; I hadn't been able to call her Mom or anything else yet.

I didn't know it was a letter at first, since it wasn't in an envelope. It was just folded sheets of paper on my brand-new bedspread under my brand-new canopy. It could have been a hate note from Holly. But as soon as I picked it up, I recognized my father's handwriting.

Sunday

Dear ~~Brooke,~~
I'm sorry I haven't written sooner. I've never been one for writing letters, ~~and this one is harder than most. It also makes me feel funny thinking about how other people are going to get to read it. But~~ I guess the judge knew what he was doing.

Things here are okay. A couple of your friends called—
Maria, and some guy, Jason, I think he said his name
was—to see how you're doing. I told them about your
message. ~~That meant a lot to me, hearing your voice. If
you ever have a chance to do it again, and it's okay, I'd
appreciate the call.~~

I've been thinking I might move. I can't decide whether
I should just get a smaller apartment—~~I don't need so
much space with you not around anymore~~—or whether
I should pack up and move someplace new. I've been
thinking about Texas. You know my restless feet. ~~If I do
get a smaller place, I'll try to save up the difference in
the rent to help you with your college expenses.~~

~~How are they treating you?~~ I watched you on TV on
Saturday ~~(Mona said I shouldn't, but I felt like I had
to),~~ and the house seemed real nice. I'm glad you're
staying at such a pretty place. ~~It makes it feel easier
somehow, seeing where you are.~~

I guess I shouldn't be telling you this, but ~~I miss you so
much, it makes~~ my teeth hurt. ~~I wake up in the
mornings and I can't believe you're gone.~~ It serves me
right, getting a taste of my own medicine. I feel real
bad about what I did to your mother. ~~I can't say any
more about it, in case she's reading this letter, but~~ I am
sorry, and I wish things had turned out different. ~~But I
love you, Brooke, and no matter what happens, they
can't take that away from me.~~

~~Sorry for sounding so maudlin. In case you've been worrying,~~ I've been to six AA meetings since you've been gone. I figure I have enough problems without adding booze to the list. And I talk to Mona a lot, and she's been a help (I know she wants to say I told you so, ~~but she's been a real lady about it and kept it to herself~~).

If there's no rule against your writing, I'd love to get a letter from you. If there is, could you ask someone to let me know ~~so I won't keep waiting to get one? Mona says she'd like to hear from you too, if you have the time. We both figure you're real busy making friends and all,~~ so we understand why you haven't written either of us yet.

Take care of yourself.

Love,
~~Dad~~

I stared at the letter, at what I could read of it, in shock. I hadn't been fantasizing about a letter, I wasn't allowing myself to fantasize about anything, but dammit, if I got one, I wanted to be able to read it. For the first time since I'd been made to live with the Girards, I felt violated and enraged and unwilling to make any effort.

The problem was if I stayed in my room and sulked, they'd know what the matter was, and that would only make things worse. I could see them notifying the judge that letters from Dad only alienated me from them and that he shouldn't be allowed any contact with me whatsoever. They'd probably even believe it. The only thing I could do with them was to be polite, swallow my anger. Otherwise Dad could move, send them my new address, and they'd never let me see it. I could go for two years without a word from him and no way of letting him know how I was. They had that power over me, and I had no power whatsoever. If I ran away, made my way back home to Dad, or even to Mona, they could change their minds about prosecuting, and Dad could end up in prison. No matter how much they claimed they loved me, in a lot of ways I was nothing more than a hostage.

So I went downstairs and I didn't say anything about the letter, and naturally they didn't either. I was a little quieter than normal, but I'd hardly been a big talker since I'd gone to live with them, and if I felt like I was being more quiet than usual, it was mostly because I knew why I wasn't speaking. If they noticed, they didn't push me on it. I went upstairs right after supper, did my homework, and stayed by myself in my fancy dream bedroom.

The next day at school I found Jessica. We had Gym together, but she hadn't made any effort to socialize with me during the week. "I want to go to the meeting," I said. "I feel real crisisy."

"Fine," Jessica said.

"I don't know where the church is," I said.

Jessica smiled. "Chris can give you a lift," she said. "He has a car. Meet him in the parking lot after school."

I wasn't sure I could make it through the school day.

I'd been there just long enough so that teachers felt I was fair game, and called on me the same as they did anybody else. Not that anyone was paying attention that day. There was a warmth in the air, the promise of spring, and on a Friday afternoon that can be fatal to concentration.

Chris had the kind of shiny red sports car that reminded me that he and Jessica and about half the other kids at that school had more money than I'd ever dreamed of seeing. I didn't care. I could match them crisis for crisis. If I needed any proof of that, I had the letter in my bag, along with my ever-present teddy bear.

"Will it be okay if I talk?" I asked him as we drove to the church.

"You can talk as much as you want," he replied. "Or as little."

"I'm really angry," I said. "About something my mother did."

Chris nodded. "We're pretty much all angry," he said. "About one thing or another."

The church was only a few blocks away from the school. I hadn't done that much exploring, but from what I could remember, it was maybe half a mile from my mother's house. I could see the church they'd gone to on Sunday a block away. I'd been made to go with them, and ordinarily that would have made me mad, but I was still on my I'm-sorry-for-all-your-pain kick and figured it was the least I could do.

A couple of the kids were already there when we arrived, and we waited a few more minutes for everyone else to show up. It turned out there were seven of us, three boys and four girls. "The number varies," Chris said, "but we usually don't have any more than ten here."

I was glad it wasn't a big group. They were strangers, after all, and I was about to pour my guts out to them. I didn't need a crowd.

"We might as well get started," Chris said. "There's a new member here today. Amy, you know Jessica, and I think you know Paul too."

I nodded. Paul was the one in my Chem class. I'd wondered on and off for a week what his problem was.

"I'm Kelly," one girl said. "And this is Shannon."

"And I'm Rick," the last kid said. "Glad you could make it, Amy."

"Hi, Amy," the others said. I said hi back, and began wondering what I was doing there.

"Does anyone mind if I go first?" Kelly asked. "I have a bitch of a weekend ahead of me, and I really could use some help."

No one stopped her.

"It's visiting weekend," she said. "Mom's making me fly out with her. She's gotten conjugal visitation rights, so I don't know why she even wants me there, but she says Dad's miserable if I don't come along. And I hate it. It may be minimum security, but they search you anyway, and it just makes me sick. How do you get through it, Chris?"

"Well, I don't have to worry about conjugal visits," he said. "That's a help."

The other kids laughed. I couldn't believe it. Half of

them had fathers in prison, and the other half thought that was funny.

"I know this isn't the same thing," Jessica said. "But when I have to go visit my father, I make believe it isn't really me."

"How do you manage that?" Kelly asked.

"I don't know," Jessica said. "It's something I've always done. It isn't like I'm a split personality or anything, but it's hard with my father, you know. I don't even know why he insists on my seeing him, I can never do anything right, and I just figured out a long time ago if I pretended I wasn't me, if I made believe I was some other girl, then when he shouts at me, it doesn't bother me as much."

"Do you do that with your mother too?" Paul asked.

Jessica shook her head. "I won't let myself," she said. "It's just for special occasions."

"So I should pretend I'm somebody else," Kelly said. "Who?"

"Sometimes I pretend I'm a reporter," Jessica said. "And I'm there to write a story."

"I could do that," Kelly said. "Is that how you handle it, Chris?"

Chris shook his head. "I only see him a couple of times a year," he said. "When I go, I tell myself it won't last too long, and it won't happen again for a while."

"You're about to turn eighteen," Paul said. "Do you think you'll keep on seeing him?"

"I don't know yet," Chris said.

"I don't understand something," I said. "Is it okay to pretend you're someone else?"

"Anything is okay if it gets you through the bad times," Jessica said.

"That isn't true," Kelly said. "Drugs aren't okay. Drinking isn't okay. Sleeping around isn't okay."

"Don't knock it until you try it," Rick said.

"That isn't funny, Rick," Paul said.

"Sorry," Rick said.

Paul turned to me. "I'm HIV positive," he said.

"How old are you?" I asked. I knew it was a dumb question, but I was so stunned, I didn't know what else to say.

"Seventeen," he said. "I don't know who infected me. If I did, I'd kill him."

He looked like he meant it. I started wondering again if I had earned my membership in this club.

"Don't you ever pretend?" Jessica asked him.

"Pretending is what got me in this mess in the first place," Paul replied. "It's better to face the truth."

"You're stronger than me," Jessica said. "No, don't deny it. Just about everybody I know is stronger than me."

"Jessica, if you weren't strong, you wouldn't be in this group," Shannon said. "You'd be off hiding somewhere, getting drunk."

"I'll never do that," Jessica said.

"That's because you're strong," Shannon said. "You do what you have to to get by."

"Do any of you drink?" I asked.

"I do," Rick said.

"I do too," Kelly said. "Paul, do you still drink?"

"Not anymore," he said. "I'm afraid it might screw up my medications."

"I miss drinking," Shannon said. "I know I can, I'm not an alcoholic or anything, but it just wouldn't be the same. Charlie and I used to drink champagne."

"How could he afford champagne on a teacher's salary?" Rick asked.

"It was domestic," Shannon said. "Charlie taught History," she said to me. "He got fired when they found out we were having an affair."

I grinned. It was comforting that someone was there because of a normal insane problem. Shannon smiled back at me, and I realized I might actually make a friend.

"How are you getting through?" Jessica asked me. "I'd think you'd be pretending all the time."

"I do sometimes," I said. "Like last night I pretended I wasn't angry. But I knew I was just acting. I still felt angry inside."

"Anger's tricky," Kelly said. "Sometimes I get so mad at my father for what he did, and what he's put us through, but there's nothing I can do about it. I mean, how can I punish him any better than the government is? So I take it out on Mom, or on Jill, and I know that isn't fair, and that makes me get angry at myself. I hate it. I hate Dad for doing this to me, and I know he never thought once about me when he was doing it. I was the last thing on his mind."

"That isn't true," Paul said. "You were the excuse.

He had to keep you and your mother and your sister in a fancy home with brand-new cars. Otherwise he never would have embezzled."

"Right," Kelly said. "Sorry. I forgot."

"Anger scares me," Chris said. "When I think about what my father did, I get terrified. Like if that kind of anger is inside me, who will I hurt?"

"You're nothing like your father," Shannon said. "I know what I'm talking about. I lived with him."

"You did?" I asked.

Shannon laughed. "My mother was his second wife," she said. "Chris and I were steps for a couple of years."

"Sometimes I think we have the worst set of fathers in the world," Jessica said. "Sometimes I wonder if there are any good fathers except on TV."

"I have a good father," I said. "Except for the fact he stole me."

"That's kind of a big fact," Kelly said.

"I didn't feel stolen," I said. "So it never bothered me."

"Did you know?" Jessica asked.

There we were, back at that question again. "I found out when I was eleven," I said.

"And you're sixteen now?" Kelly asked.

"I will be next week," I said. I was really looking forward to that birthday.

"So for five years you knew he'd snatched you and you didn't care?" Kelly asked.

"No, I didn't," I said. "I loved him. I still do. I don't know why people refuse to believe me when I say that."

"I'm sorry," Kelly said. "It's just I really love my mother, and if I knew I was being kept from her, it would drive me crazy."

"He told me she didn't want me," I said.

"But he was lying," Kelly said.

"Yeah, he was lying," I said. "First he lied to me and told me she was dead. Then he lied and said she didn't want me. I believed his lies. He was my father, and I loved him, so naturally I believed his lies."

"That's why they lie to you," Shannon said. "So you'll keep on loving them."

"That's pretty cynical," Paul said.

"It's the truth, and you know it," Shannon said. "Every time my father has a new girlfriend, which is practically once a week, he swears to me this is the one. He's finally met the right girl. My mother isn't any better. Neither one of them can look me in the eye and say, 'Hey, look, we like screwing around and we're going to keep doing it as long as our bodies will let us.' Like I'd care."

"Parents do lie," Jessica said. "My mother lies about her drinking. She always says she hasn't started again when she has. That's how I can tell. When she starts denying it, that's when she is."

"My father doesn't lie," Paul said. "The minute he found out I was gay, he said he never wanted to see me again, and he meant it."

"Yeah, but he didn't care if you loved him or not," Shannon said. "If they don't care, they don't lie."

"So lying's something positive?" Kelly asked.

"They think it is," Shannon said. "They think they're protecting us."

Jessica laughed. She looked younger when she did. She probably wasn't that much younger than I was, but I still felt those extra six months even if they'd never happened.

"I understand about protecting," I said. "I'm not even opposed to it. But now my mother wants to protect me from my father, and I don't need her to do that."

"But she doesn't know that," Kelly said.

"You know what it is," Shannon said. "You've never been divorced before."

"What do you mean?" I asked.

Shannon laughed. "You're sixteen years old, and you're going through this for the first time. God, that's got to be brutal."

"I don't get it," I said.

"My parents are divorced," Rick said. "So are Chris's and Paul's and Shannon's."

"And mine," Jessica said.

"Right," Rick said. "Sorry. The thing is, when your parents divorce, they hate each other. If they didn't, they wouldn't get the divorce in the first place."

"Sometimes they don't quite hate each other before the divorce, but then divorcing makes them hate each other," Shannon said. "Once the lawyers get involved, and they're fighting over money."

"And you're in the middle," Rick said. "Of course they pretend you aren't. They've all read the same books: 'Don't let the kids think they're to blame, never say a bad word about the other parent.' They know what they're supposed to do. They try to live up to the rules. But they always break them."

"Except my mother," Chris said. "She still won't say anything bad about Dad."

"Yeah, but that's sick too," Rick said.

"Did your father tell you bad things about your mother?" Shannon asked me.

"He said she drank and she hit me," I said. "The one time we talked about it."

"Okay, once," Shannon said. "Once, to explain why he took you, he said bad things. But he never made you feel guilty for still loving her."

"I didn't still love her," I said. "He didn't have to."

"This is gorgeous," Shannon said. "This is absolutely perfect. They have you totally unprotected."

"Who?" I asked.

"All of them," Shannon said. "Tell me. How does it feel when your mother talks about your father?"

"Like someone's playing volleyball inside me," I said.

"She is," Shannon said. "That's exactly what she's doing. It's what your father would have done if he'd had to."

"Parents want you to love them the best," Jessica said. "Even my father, and he doesn't love me at all. He's always saying bad things about my mother. Well, not directly. He asks me questions, because he knows I don't want to have to tell him the truth. It's a game they play."

"You can play it too, if you know the rules," Rick

said. "Dad lets me drive. Mom lets me stay out at night. You can tell them anything. They never check."

"But you don't know the rules yet," Shannon said. "You didn't even know they were going to play volleyball inside you."

"I can't play them against each other," I said. "It wouldn't be fair."

"Fair isn't the issue," Rick said. "Are they treating you fairly?"

The answer was no, but I couldn't make myself say it.

"Amy's situation is different from the rest of us," Paul said. "In some ways it's more like mine. There's no contact between her and her father. Right, Amy?"

"I can't see him or speak to him," I said.

"So she can't play one against the other," he said. "She can't even have that satisfaction. When my father said he never wanted to see me again, I was devastated. In some ways it was worse even than finding out I had HIV. And we had never really gotten along. Amy's lost her father. There's a barrier now between them, and it can't be crossed. I know how that feels. It isn't a game. Hell isn't a game. Not your first trip there."

"It gets easier," Shannon said. "After a while it's more comfortable hating them, and then you don't even hate them so much. You just don't care."

"It must be awful," Jessica said. "Still loving your father. Do you miss him?"

"Always," I said. It felt good to say it. "I miss him all the time. I miss my life. I miss my name and my age. I miss crying and getting angry and being able to breathe. I miss it all. I miss the lies so much."

"It's okay," Chris said. "You can cry here. You can get angry. You're among friends."

I knew he meant it. I knew it was true. I knew I was safe, and I cried.

11

April thirteenth, my second sixteenth birthday in six months, fell on a Monday. Dad and I had never made that big a deal out of birthdays, and I was hoping this one would go unnoticed.

Breakfasts at the Girards' were always chaotic with five of us fighting for bathroom space and time with the toaster. This morning wasn't any different. If my mother remembered it was my birthday, she didn't say anything about it. Under ordinary circumstances that would have seemed suspicious to me, like there was a surprise party in the works, but these were hardly ordinary circumstances. For one thing there was no one to invite to a surprise party.

School that day was better than it had been, thanks to feeling connected with the other Freaks of the Month. Shannon turned out to be in my Gym class as well as Jessica, and it felt good to have someone to joke with in the locker room. I spotted Kelly in the hallway and asked her how her weekend had gone.

"Not bad," she said. "Not great, but not bad. I tried

to pretend to be a reporter, but reality kept getting in the way."

"It has that habit," I said, and we laughed. It had been weeks since I'd laughed in a school building, weeks since I'd laughed anywhere, it felt like.

I had lunch with Chris and Jessica. "Today's my birthday," I told them. "I'm sixteen again."

"Happy birthday," Chris said.

"What does it feel like, being sixteen?" Jessica asked. "I'm going crazy waiting."

"I feel exactly the same as yesterday," I said, laughing some more. "Sixteen's just a state of mind."

"Then I must be forty," Jessica said.

"Do you have any plans?" Chris asked. "Dinner out with your family or something?"

"Not that I know of," I replied. "My mother didn't even mention it. I'm hoping she's decided not to, because of my other sixteenth birthday. Maybe she figures one a year is enough."

"Birthdays are tricky," Jessica said. "My mother always drinks harder around birthdays. Hers, mine, George Washington's."

"My father used to drink," I said. "I got a letter from him and he said he was going to a lot of AA meetings. I hope my birthday doesn't set him off."

"He probably doesn't even remember," Chris said. "When you tell yourself a lie often enough, the truth becomes kind of shadowy."

"Did you have a party the last time you were sixteen?" Jessica asked. "My mother wants to give me a party, but I keep telling her I'd rather go on a trip some-where. Somewhere without her. I haven't told her that part yet."

"Not a big party," I said. "I went out with some friends for pizza and a movie. Dad treated, but he didn't come with us." It hurt remembering back to October. "The movie wasn't that good," I said. "But we had a good time."

"We could go out after school if you want," Jessica said. "We could get pizza. Would you like that?"

"No, that's okay," I said. "I think I'll go right home."

"The important thing is not to feel sorry for your-self," Chris said.

"I know that," I said. "And I don't. It's every girl's dream to turn sixteen twice."

"It's mine to turn it once," Jessica said. "Preferably in the south of France."

"Can you afford that?" I asked.

"Probably not," Jessica said. "But why not dream the best?"

I nodded, remembering Chris's red sports car. There were people in this town with serious money. I didn't think the Girards were among them, but I wasn't sure. I used to know to the penny how much money Dad was bringing home. Every penny was budgeted. Now I had a bed with a canopy. If money bought happiness, why wasn't I smiling?

I thought about the money question some more when I walked home from school. Technically speaking, it didn't matter how much money the Girards had. If they wanted to give me room and board, fine. I didn't have any choice over that. As far as bedroom sets went, they could do what they wanted with them. The moment I could go, I was gone. Ideally that would be the day I finished high school, just one year and three months away. If not, if I had to make it through my eighteenth birthday, then okay, I would. But after that the Girards and their money were on their own.

I paused for a moment under a tree that was just starting to think about budding. Even after I graduated, I wouldn't be legally allowed to go back to Dad. If he and I were both good, and the Girards were feeling generous, then I'd get to see him by then, but that was it. I didn't know where he'd be anyway, or if he'd have space. I'd do better thinking about being on my own from the time I graduated on. I still wanted to go to college, but that might not be realistic anymore. Maybe I should think in terms of working for a couple of years and going to school at night. Of course, I had that fabulous invitation to stay with the Girards, go to college nearby, but I didn't think so. That canopy was giving me a headache.

If I was going to leave for parts unknown the day I graduated high school, then I'd better have some money saved up before then. I wasn't going to get any money from Dad, and I wasn't going to take any from the Girards. Which meant a job. Why not? If I didn't plan on going to college, what difference would it make what kind of grades I got next year?

No, that wouldn't work either. The Girards had to

not suspect anything. What I needed was a job this summer, and then I could just hold on to my money and have something to give me a head start when I graduated.

And then I had my brilliant idea. I had a job waiting for me, working as a camp counselor at the camp Mona worked at. The pay might not be fabulous, but it meant eight weeks away from the Girards. Eight weeks where nobody would know my story, where I could return to being Brooke Eastman, where I wouldn't have to watch what I said and when I sneezed and who I hated. Eight blissful, glorious, hardworking weeks, spent with kids who weren't related to me and with fellow counselors who weren't also freaks.

I felt a million times better than I had since I'd first heard about Amy Donovan. Eight weeks. If I could have eight weeks of freedom, I swore I'd be perfect for months afterward.

I walked to the Girard house humming and whistling and generally carrying on. Not even Holly's snarled hello disturbed me. Tim was in the back playing catch with his father. I made a point of stopping back there and tossing the ball around with them. There was nothing wrong with Mike and Tim. If I hadn't been related to them by blood and marriage, I probably would have liked them. And if I got to spend eight weeks away from them, who knew how I'd feel? Hell, it was amazing how much fonder I was of Charleen and her kids now that I had no opportunity to see them.

"You're in a good mood today," Mike said.

"I am," I said. "I'm in a very good mood."

"Great," he said. "That'll please your mother."

My stomach hardly clenched at all when he said that, I was so excited at the thought of not being there. I may have even smiled.

I went upstairs and did my homework so it would all be done before my mother got home from work. As soon as it was, I went downstairs and helped Mike with supper. I'd been living there two weeks, but I still didn't have any assigned jobs, other than keeping my room clean and pretending to be happy. It felt good chopping vegetables with Mike. The more I offered to help out, the more responsible they'd see I was, and the more willing they'd be to let me work away from home that summer. I'd slice and dice for months if it would get me my freedom.

My mother came home from work, and sure enough she smiled when she saw Mike and me hard at work on supper. "Is your homework done?" she asked me, just the way mothers are supposed to.

"All done," I told her.

"Great," she said. "Mike, let's use the good china tonight. It's a special occasion."

I didn't think the special occasion was the fact I'd finished my homework. But maybe it was good she remembered my birthday. Maybe she hadn't gotten me a present because she couldn't figure out what to get me and she was feeling guilt-stricken and remorseful. I didn't want her to be suicidal or anything, but a little bit of guilt could go a long way to her agreeing to my camp-counselor plan.

I took out the good china and set the table. It did

look pretty. When Mona had lived with us, she'd brought her own dishes, and we'd eaten a lot more graciously. But when she left, the dishes left also, and Dad and I had gone back to whatever wasn't broken.

I'd loved Mona and I'd loved her dishes, but I didn't remember grieving for them when they'd left. Not the dishes anyway. Not Mona either, not really, not the way she and Dad had taken to fighting. It was funny how much better she and Dad got along once they didn't have to.

Or maybe it wasn't so funny. I was feeling a lot more kindly about the Girards at the thought of not having to see them for a while.

Mike told his kids supper was ready, and we all sat down to eat. Good china meant the dining room. We sat around the table and took each other's hands. Holly dug her fingernails into me, but I just grinned.

"Dear God, thank You for Your many wonderful blessings," Mike said. "Our special thanks today for Amy's sixteenth birthday. For many years it was a dream for us, to have Amy home on her birthday, but You have made it possible. Help us be worthy of Your generosity. Amen."

"Amen," we all said. I shook my hand free of Holly.

"I was afraid you'd think we'd forgotten your birthday," my mother said as we passed the dishes among ourselves. "I should have made more of a fuss this morning."

"That's okay," I said. "I wasn't expecting presents or anything. Not after that shopping spree we went on last week."

"We have a present for you," she said. "I'm going to get it now. I can't wait."

"Shouldn't we finish supper first?" Mike asked.

"No, I'm getting it now," she said. She got up from the table, went into the kitchen, and then, as best as I could figure out, into the garage.

I have to admit it, I thought they'd bought me a car. I know it makes no sense, but Chris's red sports car popped into my mind. The Girards certainly weren't opposed to buying my love, and what better way of doing it than with a car? What did it matter that I didn't know how to drive? I could learn.

But my mother didn't carry a car back with her into the dining room. She had a shoebox instead. I laughed at myself, at my hope and my disappointment. Red sports cars would have to wait until my next lifetime.

"Happy birthday, darling," she said to me.

I took the shoebox from her. The last thing I needed was another pair of shoes. I opened the box, reminding myself that no matter what was in there, I had to look grateful. Inside was a sleeping black-and-white kitten.

"It's adorable," I said, taking the kitten out for everyone to see.

"It isn't any kind of special breed," my mother said. "I tried to find the kitten that looked most like Buttons."

"Who's Buttons?" I asked.

My mother looked stricken. "That's the cat you used to have," she said. "Don't you remember Buttons?"

Given the fact I hardly remembered her, it seemed

unlikely I'd remember the cat. "Buttons," I said. "Of course. She was so cute. She did look like this kitten."

"Buttons was a boy," Holly said. "Don't you know anything?"

"That's an easy thing to forget," Mike said. "I used to forget Buttons was a boy too. He wasn't the most macho cat I ever saw."

"This kitten's a girl, so we don't have to worry about macho," my mother said. "Amy, she's yours. You can name her whatever you want."

I almost said Brooke. The *B* sound had already started coming out when I caught myself. "Boy, I don't know," I said. "I need a really cute name."

"You said I could have a dog," Tim said.

"We never said that," his mother said.

"You did too," he said. "You said I could have a dog all my own."

"What we said was when we thought you were old enough to take care of a dog, we'd get you one," Mike said. "Maybe even next Christmas if you do all your chores and behave yourself."

"I want a dog now!" he cried.

"Yeah," Holly said. "I want a dog too."

"You don't even like dogs," her mother said.

"I do too like dogs," Holly said. "I want a dog. Timmy and I want a dog right now."

"Stop whining," her mother said.

"It isn't fair," Holly said. "Amy gets everything she wants, and Timmy and I don't get anything anymore. You don't love us now that Amy's back."

"That's not true, and you know it," Mike said. "Holly, stop acting like the world revolves around you. Today's Amy's birthday, not yours."

"Here, wait a second," I said. "Holly, why don't you take the kitten? She can be yours and I could visit her."

"No, Amy," my mother said. "That's very sweet of you, but it isn't necessary. The kitten belongs to you, not Holly."

"You see," Holly said. "She gets everything. I don't get anything."

"Holly, apologize at once to your sister," my mother said.

"She isn't my sister," Holly said.

"That does it," Mike said. "Leave the table. Go to your room, Holly, this instant."

"I bet you're going to have a big party for Amy," Holly said. "And give her everything she wants. And Timmy and me are never going to get anything."

"Timmy and I," Mike said automatically. I almost laughed, except I could see how stricken Tim looked.

"I'm not going to get a dog?" he asked.

"Timmy, I told you, maybe next Christmas," Mike said.

"But I want a dog now!" he shouted. "It isn't fair. You got Amy a cat and you won't get me a dog."

"Timmy, you're not old enough for a dog," his mother said.

"I am," Holly said. "I'm plenty old enough for a dog, but you won't get me one either. You're too busy getting things for Amy."

"I told you to go to your room," Mike said.

"My stomach hurts," Tim said.

"Fine," Mike said. "You go to your room too. Both of you, right now, and don't come out until you're willing to be members of this family again."

"I'm the member of this family," Holly said. "She's the one who isn't."

"One more word out of you and you're going to be in very serious trouble," Mike said. "Now, out, this instant!"

I watched as his children left. My mother seemed on the verge of tears. I'd never seen Mike that angry before. The only one of us who wasn't bothered by the whole scene was the kitten. She apparently could sleep through earthquakes.

"Amy, I'm sorry," Mike said. "I apologize for both Holly and Timmy. But, believe me, they'll apologize for themselves before this night is out."

"It's okay, really," I said. "This is awfully hard on them. They knew where they belonged before, and now their whole world is shot."

"They always knew they had a sister," my mother said. "You were in their prayers every night."

I bet I wasn't anymore. Not unless Holly was praying for my swift disappearance.

"Come on," Mike said. "We might as well eat supper."

"I've lost my appetite," my mother said.

"Look, I have an idea," I said. This was it, my opening. I even knew the right approach. "This adjustment hasn't been easy on any of us, I admit it, but I think it's been hardest on Holly and Tim."

"Amy, you don't have to say that," Mike said.

Oh, yes, I did. "I like them," I said. "What I mean is, I love them because they're my brother and sister and all, but I like them too. As people. You know that, Mike. Like today, when I was playing catch with you. You could tell."

"I know you've been trying with them," he said. "And I appreciate it."

"You guys have been great," I said. "There were times when I was a kid when I'd fantasize about having a family, a real one, you know, parents and brothers and sisters, but you've all been better than I could ever dream of."

"Do you mean that?" my mother asked.

I nodded. "Look, I'm not going to lie and say I'm crazy about Uncle Dick," I said. "I don't just love everybody on the spot. But the two of you, well, I know how hard you've been trying, and like I say, I *like* Holly and Tim, and I don't know if I've let you know, all of you, how grateful I am to you, but I am. For everything. The love and the understanding. The kitten. Everything."

My mother was eating it up. I wasn't that sure about Mike though, and the kitten woke up long enough to give me a long, skeptical yawn.

"So here's my idea," I said. "One that might make the adjustment easier on Holly and Tim."

"We're listening," Mike said.

I smiled at him. "I thought maybe this summer I could get a job as a camp counselor," I said.

"Absolutely not," he said.

"You don't understand," I said. "I wouldn't have to job-hunt or anything. I was supposed to work at a camp . . . a camp I know about." I almost mentioned Mona, but I thought better of it. "It's the camp I used to go to. It was all arranged."

"You want to spend the summer there?" my mother asked.

"It would be fun," I said. "I was really looking forward to it, and it was all arranged, so it would be really convenient. Of course I'd miss all of you, but it would give Holly and Tim more of a chance to adjust to me."

"I don't see how they could adjust to you better if you weren't around," Mike said. "The idea is for them to get to know you, not avoid you."

"It would give them some breathing room," I said. "Some time for the four of you together, the way it used to be."

"No," my mother said. "I forbid it."

"But why?" I asked.

"I don't like the sound of it," my mother said. "If it's the camp you used to go to, Hal must know about it. How do we know he won't try to contact you while you're there?"

"This isn't about him," I said. "I don't want to spend the summer there to see Dad." Damn. I probably wasn't supposed to call him that.

"Why do you want to spend the summer there, then?" Mike asked.

To get away from all of you, I thought. *To earn some*

money for my escape. To be someplace where I could be called Brooke. "For all our sakes," I said. As answers go, that one was almost honest.

My mother shook her head. "I didn't wait eleven long years to have you leave home two months later," she said. "We're spending this summer together as a family. I've already applied for four weeks' leave. We're going to go on a trip together, to the Grand Canyon and Yosemite. Disneyland. It's going to be a dream trip."

"You can afford that?" I asked.

My mother looked guilty.

"What?" I said. "What's going on?"

"We've been approached by the TV company that produces *Still Missing*," Mike said. "They want to buy the rights to our story for a TV movie."

"A TV movie about me?" I said.

"Not just about you," he said. "About all of us. Your mother's search for you all these years. The community effort. What it did to Holly and Timmy."

"But let me guess how it ends," I said. "With me calling the eight-hundred number, right? With our reunion?"

"What's wrong with that?" my mother asked. "If our story could give hope to some other mother out there whose ex-husband stole her children the way Hal did mine, she could know there are happy endings if you work and you pray hard enough. I think it's a wonderful idea."

"I think it stinks," I said. "Dammit, how often does the world have to hear all about me? Wasn't twice enough?"

"We told you to watch your language in this house," Mike said. "Your cursing is not appreciated."

"I'm sorry," I said real fast. "I really am. I just wasn't expecting any of this. Not the kitten or the fight or the trip or being on TV again."

"We know how hard all this has been on you," Mike said. "And we've been trying our best to make it as easy as we can."

"How about we compromise?" I asked. "Make the TV movie, give hope to all those mothers, but let me work as a counselor this summer. Any camp you want. Any sleepaway camp, I mean."

"No," my mother said.

"Apparently you don't understand," Mike said. "The decisions your mother and I make are with your best interests in mind. We know what's best for you, and what's best for you this summer is a family trip across country."

I knew why too. If Dad moved and we were away from home, we'd never be able to find each other. "Are we going to come back?" I asked.

"Of course we are," my mother said. "What kind of question is that?"

"I don't know," I said. "I just wondered."

"Let me explain something to you," Mike said. "If your mother wanted, we could leave this town, move anywhere in the United States, and have no moral or legal obligation to tell Hal where we went. But we aren't about to do that. No matter how badly he hurt us, we're not out to hurt him back."

"Is that what you thought?" my mother asked. "That

this trip is some kind of a scheme to keep you and your father apart?"

"I don't know," I said. "Yeah. Maybe."

"We don't need schemes," she said. "The judge ruled that you're mine, not Hal's. The only reason he isn't in jail right now is because Mike convinced me it would be too hard on you. None of this is about Hal. He can't even see you for another two years. And by then you're going to be a full-fledged member of this family. You'll know what real love is, and you won't want to have anything more to do with him. I swear that to you, Amy. Just give us a little time for you to find out what love is really all about."

I nodded. The kitten woke up and purred. *She knew what love was all about,* I thought. Maybe she could teach me.

12

I got home from school on Thursday to find Holly and Tim all alone. That happened sometimes, although Mike usually got out of school about forty minutes before his kids did and was likely to be there when they got in.

I was used to being home alone after school and found the presence of so many people smothering. Fortunately after the first week my mother had gone back to her full-time job, and she didn't get home until after five.

Holly and Tim had apologized to me Monday night, and I'd accepted their apologies with as much sincerity as they'd offered. That isn't fair really. Tim didn't know what he was apologizing for, and since I wasn't sure myself, sincerity didn't enter into it. Holly, on the other hand, didn't mean a word of it, but at least she said what she was supposed to, and her parents accepted the gesture at face value. I wasn't about to argue. I wasn't about to argue anything anymore. The Girards had me, I was stuck, there was no going back and not much going forward either.

When I got home from school on Thursday, the kitten, at least, was pleased to see me. She'd accidentally got shut into my bedroom and was frantic for release. I couldn't blame her. But I could blame Holly, who must have heard the kitten's piteous wailing when she went to her own bedroom. Not to mention my room's new fragrance, essence of kitten trapped for hours without a litter box.

I considered dumping the kitten's gift package on Holly's bed. She didn't have a canopy, so it would undoubtedly air out faster than it was going to in my room, but I knew that would be petty, mean-spirited, and just a little too much fun for me to get away with. Instead I waved good-bye to the kitten, who raced in search of food and other necessities, cleaned off the bedspread as best I could, and cursed my existence. In other words a fairly typical day in the life of Amy Donovan.

Tim was downstairs when I went down. He was sitting in the living room watching TV. Holly was by his side.

"Want to play catch, Tim?" I asked him.

His face lit up. "Okay," he said.

"Why do you do that?" Holly asked.

"Do what?" I asked.

"Call him Tim," she said. "His name is Timmy."

I realized then I didn't know what Tim's name was. I'd assumed Timothy, but no one had told me, or told me his or Holly's middle names. I had one, so they probably did, but apparently I was just supposed to know them.

"You know," I said to Holly, because I was actually amused by this and there was no one else to tell it to, "I don't know Tim's name. His full name, I mean."

"His full name is Timmy," Holly said.

I thought about it. I was Amy, and she was Holly, so maybe he really was Timmy. But that didn't seem very Mikeish to me. "Tim, what's your real name?" I asked him.

"Timothy David Girard," he said.

"Thank you," I said. "Want to play catch, Timothy David Girard?"

"Sure, Amy Michelle Girard," he said. He thought that was very funny, and laughed at his own joke.

"Her name isn't Girard," Holly said. "It's Donovan, same as her no-good father."

"I don't understand," Tim said. "Why isn't her name Girard? Mom says she's our sister."

"She isn't our full sister," Holly said. "You and I are full sisters. Sisters and brothers. You know what I mean. Dad's our dad and Mom's our mom. But Amy's father is no good. You know that. He's the man who broke Mom's heart and made her cry all those years. Amy's just like him too. She makes Mom cry all the time."

"I do not," I said. "And my father's plenty good. You just don't know him."

Tim shook his head. "Your father is a very bad man," he said. "I know because Mommy says so."

"Fine," I said. "He's a terrible man. But he taught me how to play catch, which I'm still willing to do."

"Okay," Tim said.

"No," Holly said. "Timmy, don't you play catch with her." She made *her* sound like a disease.

"Why not?" Tim and I both asked.

"Because she learned how from her father," Holly said. "You just heard her say that."

This was twisted even from Holly. "What difference does it make who I learned catch from?" I said. "Catch is catch. You throw the ball, and the other person catches it."

"How do I know you won't hurt Timmy?" Holly asked.

"What?" I said.

"Maybe you'll throw the ball right at his head," she said. "People do that all the time."

"Fine," I said. "You're right. You're absolutely right. I was planning on throwing the ball at Tim's head until he died. Or at least until he got a major-league headache like the one you give me all the time."

"Did you hear that, Timmy?" Holly said. "I told you she was bad. She wants to kill you."

"She's right," I said. "You know those stomachaches you keep having?"

Tim nodded.

"I've been poisoning your food," I said. "I've been putting arsenic in it. You first, then Holly, and then your stupid parents. If that all works out, I'll try for the president next."

Tim stared at me, and then he ran upstairs.

"Can't you take a joke?" I called after him, but apparently he couldn't.

"You scared him," Holly said.

"Well, it was your fault," I said, "suggesting I'd want to hurt him."

Holly gave me another of her scathing you-are-trash-and-I-despise-you looks. She had a thousand of them, different varieties for different occasions. "You do want to hurt him," she said. "You want to hurt all of us because you hate us."

Holly had a point. I did want to hurt all of them. Not all of them all the time, but at least one of them at some time. Most of the time I liked Mike, and I almost always liked Tim, but Mike I hadn't particularly cared for on Monday, and Tim was annoying me plenty just then. I alternated between feeling sorry for my mother and loathing her, and with Holly I didn't even have to alternate.

The TV was still tuned to some dumb cartoon show. I turned it off. "Could we talk?" I asked Holly. "I mean seriously talk."

"About what?" she asked.

"I don't know," I said. "About how we're sisters, maybe."

"I don't want to be your sister," she said. "I hate you."

"Fine, I understand that," I said. "There's no reason why you should like me. I barge into your house, I take over the den, I get all kinds of presents and a kitten, and everybody pays attention to me. That must be hell on you."

"You aren't nice," Holly said. "You're just like your father. Mom always said when you'd come back, you'd be so happy and you'd love all of us and you'd be just like us, but you aren't. You don't belong here. You belong with your no-good father."

"You know that and I know that, but the judge didn't care," I said. "I'm stuck here, and you're stuck with me."

"No, I'm not," Holly said. "I'm going to run away."

I was tempted to pack her bag. "No, you're not," I said instead. "Because you love your . . . parents, both of them, and you don't want to hurt them. You want her to start crying all the time again?"

"If I run away, it'll all be your fault," Holly said. "And then they'd have to send you back."

I considered it. Was it worth a try? Probably not. "I don't think so," I said. "They're pretty determined to keep me. I think if you ran away, they'd just find you and get mad, punish you somehow. Ground you, or no TV, or something like that. Whatever it is they do."

Holly looked at me. "I hate you," she said, and she began to cry.

"I know, kid," I said, searching around for tissues. I spotted a box on an end table and brought it over to her. She used about a half dozen of them before she was through.

"I still hate you," she said. "Do you hate me?"

"Yeah," I said. "I do."

"And Mommy and Daddy and Timmy?" she asked.

"I hate everything and everybody right now," I said.

"Do you hate your father?" she asked.

"He's the only one I don't hate, dammit," I said.

"You shouldn't curse," Holly said. "There's a rule."

"I hate rules too," I said. It felt good being honest in that house. "I hate rules and bedroom sets and . . . I don't know what else. . . . Suburbs. I hate suburbs."

"Do you hate boys?" she asked.

"Well, no, now that you mention it," I said. "There was this boy at my old school, Jason Best, and I really liked him, and he liked me too, I think. He called my dad after I left."

"Do you like any boys here?" Holly asked.

"I don't know," I said. "It's hard for me to like anything here. I know you hate me, and I know you don't care, but this has really been awful on me, Holly."

"When I was little, I wanted a big sister," Holly said. "My friend Jamie had a big sister, and she was really nice to us. She let us play with her makeup and everything. And I told Mommy I wanted a big sister, and she cried. She said I knew I had one, and someday she'd come back and live with us. And I said, 'Will she be nice like Jamie's big sister?' and Mommy said she'd be even better, because she'd be just like us, and she'd be so happy to be home. But I wasn't sure, you know. I knew how nice Jamie's big sister was, and she was the one I wanted. And then I felt bad, because Mommy wanted you back so much, and I wanted a big sister, but I didn't want you. And I couldn't tell her that. So every night when I'd pray for you, after Mommy and Daddy left my room, I'd pray that when you came back, you'd be just like Jamie's big sister. Sometimes I prayed that Jamie's big sister was really you and Jamie's family had somehow gotten her by mistake. I know that's dumb, but I was little."

"I bet I was a real disappointment," I said.

"Well, you aren't Jamie's big sister," Holly said.

"That's probably for the best," I said. "Amy and Jamie. It sounds a little weird."

Holly laughed.

"What's your middle name?" I asked.

"Don't you remember?" Holly asked. "You named me."

"I did?" I said.

She nodded. "Daddy told me. When I was born, he took you to the hospital to meet me, and he told you my name was Christine Holly Girard, and you said no, call me Holly first, so they did. I mean Christine Holly's on my birth certificate, but that's why everybody calls me Holly. Because you made them."

"God," I said. "I mean gosh. I hope you don't mind."

"I like it," Holly said. "There are three other girls in my class named Christine, but I'm the only Holly. You don't remember that, naming me Holly?"

I shook my head.

"Are you sure you're really Amy?" Holly asked. "Wouldn't it be great if you really weren't?"

"We shouldn't count on it," I said. "Dad said I am, and he should know."

"Maybe he just wanted to get rid of you," Holly suggested.

"No," I said. "He didn't."

"Oh," she said. "Do you think you're ever going to like us?"

"I'm not sure," I said. "I like you more than I did ten minutes ago."

"I still hate you," Holly said.

"That's fine," I told her. "I bet Jamie hates her big sister sometimes too."

"You don't mind that I hate you?" Holly asked.

"I mind, I guess," I said. "Sure I mind. But I understand." I was silent for a moment and stared at the blank TV screen. "You know, my father married this woman named Mona," I said. "I really loved her, so I didn't mind. I was glad. But then I found out Mona was trying to have a baby. At first I was excited. I thought it'd be fun having a baby in the house. I think I may have even remembered you then, how excited I was about you, but I'm not sure. I can't remember anymore what I actually felt or what I think I ought to have felt instead. But I do remember being excited about having a baby around, until one night I got scared."

"Scared of a baby?" Holly asked.

"Scared they'd love the baby more than me," I said. "Mona wasn't my mother. She was bound to love her own baby more than me. She probably wasn't going to love me at all once the baby came. And Dad and I had been alone together for a long time, but he had Mona now, and I knew it was hard for him raising me. Sometimes he even told me so. And I had this friend—well, she was only ten —but she'd been kicked around a lot, and she said when Dad and Mona had the baby, they'd probably get rid of me. I'd end up with foster parents."

"Did you believe her?" Holly asked.

"I wasn't sure," I said. "And I was too scared to ask Dad and Mona. I was scared a lot. I was scared about a lot of things I never told anybody about."

"Did they have the baby?" Holly asked.

I shook my head. "Mona couldn't," I said. "So she told Dad she wanted them to adopt, and that's when Dad told her they couldn't, because of me. Because my mom wasn't really dead, and he didn't have legal custody of me, and that's why we'd changed our names and moved around so much. I was eleven. I wasn't supposed to hear it, but I did. I overheard a lot of things when I was eleven I wasn't supposed to."

"I eavesdrop too," Holly said. "They whisper all the important stuff."

"I don't want you to hate me," I said. "And I don't want Tim to be scared of me. I feel awful for him, the way his stomach hurts all the time."

"His stomach always hurts," Holly said. "It hurt before you got here."

"Even so," I said. "I think I'm going to go upstairs and tell him I'm sorry I scared him."

"Okay," she said.

I got up off the sofa and turned the TV back on for her. "And I'm sorry I've been mean to you," I said. "I'll try to be better." I paused for a moment and remembered my dad. "No, I won't try," I said. "I will be better. I promise."

"Okay," Holly said, but she was looking at the TV. I didn't blame her. It felt good not to for a change.

I went to Tim's room and found him lying on his

bed. "I came up here to apologize," I said. "I wasn't going to hurt you, and it was mean of me to say I was. Do you forgive me?"

"I knew you weren't going to," he said. "I knew you were kidding."

"Still want to play catch?" I asked him.

"Sure," he said. "Wait. Let me get my glove."

I waited while he dug his glove and ball out from under the rubble. We went downstairs and out by the kitchen door and threw the ball around for almost an hour. When Mike got in, he joined us. I felt comfortable there. It was easier with them. I was more used to men, to boy talk. I'd played catch a lot more often than dolls when I was a kid.

We stopped playing when we saw the car drive up with my mother. We helped her carry the bags of groceries into the house.

"Holly, come in here and help me put things away," she said.

"Oh, Mother," Holly said.

I think my mother caught the normalcy in Holly's voice. "Oh, Mother," she parroted, sounding exactly like her daughter.

The pain hit me then. It was funny, no matter how often I was stabbed by pain, it always felt unexpected. This time it came from nothing, from a simple mother-daughter exchange. I knew those tones though, because I might not have had a mother, but my friends all did, and I'd heard them say "Oh, Mother," or the equivalent, and I'd heard their mothers say the same right back at them. I hadn't been jealous of them. Most of my friends had been jealous of me, thinking it was glamorous somehow to live alone with your father, the way so many kids did on TV. I hadn't been jealous of them for having mothers, because I just didn't, like I didn't have a pony. First she was dead and then she didn't love me, but either way she didn't exist for me, and I was never going to have a pony and I was never going to have a mother.

But Holly did. Cranky, miserable, jealous Holly had the one thing my father had made sure I would never have. She had a mother she could shout at and be mean to and cry in front of and let her know just how scared she was. Holly had all that and I didn't, and there was only one reason why I didn't. One reason why I had never known the love and the security of a mother. One reason why I hadn't even allowed myself to be upset when Mona left us, because that's what mothers did, they loved you for a little while maybe, but then they stopped and it was a good thing you had Dad, because he'd always love you. One reason why I didn't belong in my own home, and probably never would. One goddamn stinking son-of-a-bitch reason, and that was the only person, I kept telling myself, that had ever really loved me. That goddamn stinking son of a bitch. What the hell could he know about love?

13

Rick wasn't at the Freak-of-the-Month Club meeting the next day, and a different boy, Craig, who I recognized from a couple of my classes, was. I didn't care. I was so angry at that point I would have shouted my problems at Yankee Stadium.

I didn't even mind waiting my turn; it just fed my rage. I liked feeling this angry. It was the right way to feel, the way I'd been denying myself during this whole miserable mess.

Craig finished with his problems, which were familiar to everyone else and of no interest to me, and before anybody else had a chance, I said, "I have a lot of stuff I need to talk out."

"Hard week?" Shannon asked.

"They're all hard," I said. "No, that isn't it. I mean, it is, but that's not what I need to talk about."

I waited for somebody to interrupt, make a wisecrack, grab the attention, but nobody did. They were all listening to me. They didn't care, not the way real friends do, but they cared enough to listen, and I was grateful.

"Everybody keeps asking me about Dad," I said. "About what he told me and why I believed his lies. And I told everybody the same thing, that it didn't matter, that I love him and he raised me and so what if he lied. I meant it too. But yesterday I had a glimpse of what his lies cost me. Just a taste of it, you know, nothing big, but God, it hurt so much. All I do lately is hurt, but this one set the record."

"What happened?" Jessica asked.

"It was nothing," I said. "I think that's why it hurt so much. All of you, whether you like them or not, you have two parents. You know what you can count on them for, good or bad. I never had that, so I told myself I didn't need it. I didn't need a mother. I didn't need a family. I didn't need a hometown. As long as I had Dad, I didn't need anything else. And yesterday, for the first time, it hit me. He stole all that from me. I don't know what kind of mother she is. Maybe she stinks. But I never had the chance to know. I have this half sister and half brother, and we don't get along very well, especially my half sister and me, and maybe we never would have, but there's no way of knowing anymore. We might have been close. I might have loved her and been proud of her. I didn't even know Tim existed. You should know if you have a brother. That's an important thing. And he stole it from me. He stole my entire goddamn childhood, and he substituted another one, and all this time I've been telling myself I'm Brooke Eastman, and this Amy Donovan business, that's the charade, but who knows? If you're brought up on nothing but lies, maybe all you are is a lie."

"I don't think so," Kelly said. "Everybody's parents lie."

"I know those lies," I said. " 'It won't hurt.' 'Try it once, you'll like it.' 'Someday you'll look back on all this and laugh.' I'm not talking about lies like that. I'm talking about being told your mother is dead when she's alive, being told she doesn't want you when she's searching for you day and night, being told your birthday's in October when it's actually in April, being told we're moving so he can get a better job, when actually we're moving so the law won't find us. Those kinds of lies. They're part of me. And I hate them, and I hate him for telling me them and making me not a real person, not the person I really should be."

"Dammit," Jessica said.

We all looked at her.

"Remember last week?" she said. "I said we all had terrible fathers, and Amy said she didn't. Now she says she does. I liked the idea that somebody had a good father. That meant something to me."

"Tell me about it," I said.

"I'm not sure I totally understand this," Shannon said. "You're mad at your father, that I get. But do you want to be close now to your mother?"

"I don't know," I said. "I don't know if I can be. She looks in on me at night to make sure I'm still there. I can't breathe around her. Do you ever feel that way about your mothers?"

"I do sometimes," Chris said. "It's a kind of overprotectiveness. They don't mean any harm by it."

"It drives me crazy," I said. "It's another thing I have to hate Dad about. If he'd just left me with her, she wouldn't worry so much about me. She'd know me, just like I'd know her. Dammit, I really want to kill him."

"Have you told him how you feel?" Paul asked.

"I can't," I said. "He isn't allowed to call me, and I don't dare call him from their house. It's a long-distance call; they'd know I made it. And I can't write to him, because he can't write back without her reading the letter. That's the whole idea, keeping him from me. That's his punishment. They don't care that it's mine too, because not a single, solitary one of them really cares about me."

Chris cleared his throat. "Self-pity, Amy," he said.

"Screw you," I said. "If I don't have the right, who does?"

"Me first," Shannon said.

"No, I want to go first," Jessica said.

"I have all of you beat," Paul said. "I'm terminal."

"Oh, God," I said. "Protect me from freaks."

Everyone laughed. I did too. It felt good to be inside a laugh, to be part of a joke, and not its butt.

"Okay," I said. "You're right, Chris. I am feeling sorry for myself. And angry at the world. It's not a pretty picture."

"It's an understandable one though," Shannon said. "I feel sorry for myself all the time, Amy. It's how I get through the day. Chris just likes being stoic. He thinks girls go for that."

"What I think is self-pity is a waste of time," Chris

said. "And none of us have that much time to waste. Paul's taught me that."

"Always glad to be of help," Paul said. "Amy, you've got to talk to your father."

"But I can't," I said.

"You have to," he said. "Chris is right. Self-pity is a waste of time. But so's festering anger. You said you want to kill your father. I don't know if you mean it or not, but I do know I'd like to kill mine. It eats at me day and night, what he said about me, how he refuses to see me. I don't expect teary reconciliations. I don't even want them. He can't stand my guts, fine. He doesn't deserve me, I'm too damn good for him. But I'd like to tell him what I think. I'd like him to have just a taste of my anger. And I live with that rage inside me, and sometimes when I should be thinking about Chemistry, or who's going to win the pennant, or what can I do with whatever time I have left, instead the rage takes over. I don't care how you do it, Amy, but you have to let him know how you feel."

"Call from my house," Chris said.

"What?" I said.

"When we're through here, I'll drive you to my house," he said. "My mother won't notice one more long-distance call. If she does, I'll just pay for it out of my allowance."

"He won't be home," I said. "He'll be at work."

"Then leave a message," Chris said. "Does he have the kind of machine you can leave a long message on?"

I nodded.

"Then tell him exactly what you think," he said.

"Maybe it won't be as good as telling him to his face, or even having him on the other end, but it's something. You'll feel better."

"That's a great idea," Jessica said. "It'll be even better than talking to him, because he won't be able to excuse himself. You can picture him listening to your message. You can tell him exactly what you think of him, and he won't have any way of getting back at you." She paused for a moment. "Gee, that sounds great," she said. "I'd love to do that with my father."

"Yours would call back," Kelly said. "He'd put you on hold for a while, but he'd call back."

"I know," Jessica said. "But I can dream."

"Dreaming helps," Kelly said, but I'd already stopped focusing on them and had started thinking about just what I would say to Dad. To him. To my father. To no-good Hal Donovan.

The meeting broke up close to five. After a while I'd been able to concentrate on everyone else and had even participated in the conversations. It felt good to be part of a group. Back at my old high school my friend Maria had belonged to three different clubs, and she was always after me to join one, but I'd never really wanted to, since I never was sure I'd be staying much longer. Turned out I was right on that one.

Chris drove me back to his house in his flashy red sports car. His house turned out to be nice and old and enormous. "God, you *are* rich," I said.

He blushed. "My mother is," he said. "Don't hold it against me."

"I don't care," I said. "Do you make a lot of long-distance phone calls?"

"I make a lot," he said. "I have a lot of friends all over the place. People I've met and liked and stayed in touch with."

"I bet you do," I said.

"Did you do that?" he asked. "Stay in touch with your friends when you moved?"

"Dad didn't want me to," I said. "So I never bothered."

"Well, that's changed now," he said. "Use the phone in my room. You can close the door, and no one will hear you."

"Who's no one?" I asked.

"Just me and Juanita," he said. "The housekeeper. Today's my mother's volunteer day at the museum. She won't be home before eight."

"Great," I said. "Thanks a lot."

"It's okay," he said. "Take your time. Curse all you want."

I smiled at him. "I'm going to use words you never knew existed," I told him.

"Just as long as your father knows what they mean," Chris said. "My room is the first door on the right upstairs. I'll be downstairs in the den if you need me."

"Thanks again," I said. I walked up the stairs, admiring the paintings that hung on the hall walls, and found his bedroom right away. It had a boy's room look to it. A boy with money, maybe, but still a boy.

I took a moment to think about how I'd felt yesterday watching Holly and my mother, letting the rage soak back into me, getting back that feeling of terror at abandonment, getting back that feeling of expecting nothing else. I closed my eyes and made myself feel five again, tried to remember just what it was like knowing my mommy was dead. It was easier to be eleven and hear that she wasn't dead, that that was a lie to protect me because she didn't want to have anything to do with me. She didn't think I was good enough for her. As soon as Dad had told me that, I had known Mona would leave me. If I wasn't good enough for my own mother, how could I possibly expect anybody else to love me?

It came back to me. It was always there, always part of me, of Brooke Eastman, of the lie I'd grown up being. And so was my hate for my father. It was an old friend, just waiting to be let in, and I opened the door and let it embrace me.

I dialed his number. He'd get a message he'd never forget.

"Hello?"

"Wait a second," I said. "Dad, you're home?"

"God, Brooke, is that you? Where are you? Are you all right?"

"Why aren't you at work?" I asked. Dammit, how could he just answer the phone like that?

"I quit my job a couple of days ago," he said. "I wrote you I was thinking about moving. Did you get my letter? I wasn't sure she'd let you read it."

"I got it," I said. "I hadn't realized you'd be moving so soon."

He laughed. "It's felt like a lifetime, honey," he said. "The past couple of weeks have been an eternity."

"Oh," I said. "I just thought I'd leave you a message."

"You have no idea how happy I am to hear your voice," he said. "But where are you calling from? Is everything okay?"

"Yeah, it is," I said. "I'm not sick or anything."

"So you're calling, like, from school," he said. "Just to let me know. God, I'm glad you did. Are you at a pay phone? Give me the number, and I'll call you right back."

"No, that's okay," I said. "I'm at a friend's house."

"I knew you'd be making friends," he said. "You always had a gift for that. You settling in all right? Are they treating you okay?"

"They're doing their best," I said. "So am I."

"That's good," he said. "You know, tell you the truth, this time I didn't quit. I got fired. I couldn't concentrate on my job anymore. I was thinking about you all the time, worrying about you. I kept goofing up. My boss calls me in to fire me and I had to tell him I didn't blame him. I would have fired me too. He was so surprised, he wrote me this really good letter of recommendation. Of course I told him I was thinking about quitting anyway, moving to Texas. I told him you'd gone to live with your mother, so there was no reason to stay on here. Turned out he's getting a divorce, so he was pretty sympathetic. Nicest firing I ever had." He laughed.

"Dad," I said.

"You're right," he said. "This is your dime, not mine.

How are you? How's school? Are you having trouble adjusting to the different classes?"

"School's okay," I said. "Dad, I called you because there's something I have to say to you."

"I'm listening," he said.

I knew he was too. I could see him concentrating on me. It had always seemed that way to me, that no matter how trivial my words were, he cared enough to really listen. Once again I could feel his love for me. Once again I felt that eternal volleyball game being played inside me.

"Dad, you shouldn't have lied to me," I said. I'd start with a simple statement of fact.

"I know," he said. "I'm sorry."

"No," I said. "That isn't enough. You can't just apologize. You hurt me. You hurt me really bad."

There was silence on his end.

"I look at her and she isn't my mother," I said. "Because I don't know what a mother is. I ought to, Dad. I had one. I had a mother who loved me, and you took me from her and never let me know her. That was cruel, Dad. You always said I should never be cruel, and you were as cruel as they come. God only knows how much you hurt her. I don't even care right now. All that matters to me this minute is how you hurt me."

I could hear him crying. I'd always hated that, when he cried, because it had scared me so. If he wasn't strong, what did I have? Now I was glad he was crying. I hoped he'd never stop.

"I don't understand how you could have done it to me," I said. "You were always telling me how much you loved me. I even believed it. I believed it for a long time. But if you'd really loved me, you would have let me know my mother. You wouldn't have cheated me. How could you do that? How could you tell me you loved me when you were hurting me so bad?"

"Oh, Brooke," he said.

"Call me Amy!" I shouted. "That's my goddamn name."

"Brooke, Amy," he said. "What do you want me to do? Do you want me to kill myself? Believe me, I've been thinking about it. Maybe it's the best thing I could do for you."

"Oh no you don't," I said. "For eleven years you kept me from having a mother. You're not going to keep me from having a father now. You're not going to get off that easy."

He was sobbing now. So what? I'd done my share of sobbing lately. My mother had certainly done hers over the years. I imagined all the things my mother must have wanted to say to him, and for the first time I appreciated her restraint.

"I hate you," I said. "And I don't know if I'm ever going to stop hating you."

"Brooke, don't, please," he said.

I could picture him fragmenting in front of me, shattering into a thousand tiny pieces. I watched him smash over and over again until I lost pleasure at the image. "Go wash your face," I said. "There's still stuff I need to say."

"Hold on," he said. I could hear him walk away from the phone and run the water. He'd always made me wash my face with cold water after I'd been crying. He never made me stop, just suggested that when I was through, I wash my face. It used to work too. When I'd fall and hurt myself, he'd kiss the bruise, and that worked too. Had my mother done that? Probably. I probably hadn't been allowed to remember it, that's all.

"I'm back," he said. "I'm sorry, Brooke. About breaking down that way. And don't worry. I'm not going to do anything stupid. More stupid, I mean. I shouldn't have said that."

"No, you shouldn't have," I said.

"I get scared," he said. "I know I'm your dad, you think of me as a big person, someone who can take care of himself, but the kind of scared I get, I'm just a little kid inside. I never wanted that for you. I don't know. I've probably cursed you forever, and that was the last thing I ever wanted for you."

"I just don't understand," I said. "How could you love someone as much as you say you love me and hurt me this way?"

"Good question," he said, and he took a deep breath. "No easy answer."

"Then give me a hard one," I said. "I have to know, Dad. I have to know how much to hate you."

"Fair enough," he said. "Hard answers. God, you'd think I'd know what to tell you. I haven't thought about much else since they took you."

"Start with the beginning," I said. "You told me she hit me. She didn't, did she, Dad? That was your first lie."

"No, that was the truth," he said. "She did. The

thing is though, I did too. It's real easy to hit a kid when you need to hit something and the kid's right there. She used to hit you, not so bad you'd end up in the hospital or anything, but bad enough so I could tell, and I hated that. I used to get hit when I was a kid, and I always swore no kid of mine would ever be treated that way, and there you were, and it drove me crazy."

"You're not lying?" I asked.

"I don't blame you for not believing me," he said. "But that much is true. Maybe I should have done something else about it. It's pretty obvious what I did was wrong, just snatching you that way. I should have called Social Services or something, but I was scared you'd end up in a foster home somewhere. I didn't want that for any kid of mine either. So I took you. Later on, when I was hitting you, I felt bad. I mean, what was I saving you from? You weren't any better off if I was the one batting you around. You were worse off, just because I was stronger. I told myself it was the booze, and I started AA, and maybe it was. I know once I stopped drinking, I stopped hitting. Maybe your mother had been drinking too. Maybe that's why she'd been hitting you. I don't know. I wasn't there. We split up when you were a baby. I was lucky to have any kind of visitation rights at all, you were so young. But, God, I loved you. I used to dream about having a family when I was a kid, and once you were born, I swore nothing and no one was going to keep us apart. Not the court. Not your mother. Nothing. You were my family. You were all I had."

"And that's why you took me?" I asked. "Because I was all you had?"

"I guess," he said. "Mike, that stepfather of yours, he was making noises like he wanted to adopt you. He was a decent guy, even I could see that, and you were crazy about him. You called him your new daddy. I don't know. I probably should have just gotten married again, had a whole new family, but you looked like me. Even when you were a baby. And you had a way of looking at me, like I was the most important thing on earth. You told me once I was better than ice cream. I'll never forget that. Better than ice cream."

"So you took me because you were afraid of losing me," I said.

"More than anything else," he said. "That's why I took you."

"But you made me lose my mother," I said. "That was the price I had to pay."

"I knew it was wrong," he said. "From day one I knew it was a mistake. You used to cry every night after I told you your mommy was dead. It broke my heart to hear you crying yourself to sleep. I thought about bringing you back, but I knew if I did, they'd never let me see you again, and I couldn't stand that. I'd grown up without a mother. I knew it could be done. I told myself I'd be mother and father to you. I'd be the best damn parent that ever walked the face of this earth. I'd go to your recitals and know your friends on sight and make sure you grew up straight and proud."

"You did a good job," I said. "When we weren't running."

"Nobody's perfect," he said.

"All right," I said. "I understand why you lied to me when I was little. But then when I overheard you and Mona talking, why did you tell me my mother didn't want me? How could you do that to me? Do you have any idea how much that hurt me?"

"That was the worst thing I've ever done in my life," he said. "Worse than snatching you even. Worse than what I did to your mother when we were married. Worse than hitting you."

"But you did it anyway," I said.

"It was the fear," he said. "If you knew the truth, you'd stop loving me. I wouldn't have blamed you. I don't blame you now. But by lying to you I bought myself five years of your love. It isn't fair. I know it, and I'm sorry like you wouldn't believe. But that's why I did it. You know the truth, you're out of there on the next bus."

"Were you ever going to tell me?" I asked. "Or was I supposed to hate her until the day I died?"

"I kept telling myself I would," he said. "Tell you the truth on your twelfth birthday. Then on your fourteenth. On your sixteenth. The day you graduated high school. The day you went off to college. The day you got married. The day I died. There was always going to be one right day to let you know what I'd done to you, but that day never seemed to come."

"I'm glad I called the eight-hundred number," I said, and for the first time ever I meant it.

"Good," he said. "You took that bus. You're where you belong."

"I don't want to forgive you," I said. "Not for a long time. I want to know you're in pain."

"Don't worry, honey," he said. "I am."

"I don't want to lose you either," I said. "I can't. I can't bear that idea. It kills me inside, that you might snatch yourself the way you snatched me, that you might disappear into Texas or Alaska or Australia or someplace."

"I won't disappear," he said. "Not ever. You're all I have, Brooke. You're my world."

"I know," I said. "I've loved you for an awfully long time, Dad. I'm not going to stop. But I don't think I'll ever love you that same way again."

He was crying again. Not sobs this time, but a soft, gentle crying.

"Oh, Daddy," I said. He used to say "Oh, baby," to me in that exact same voice when I was the one who couldn't stop crying.

"I'm sorry," he said. "You'll never know how sorry."

I didn't want to know either. It was enough to know how scared he was, how scared he'd always been. If I was that scared of losing him, when I had a mother and a stepfather and a sister and a brother and an aunt and an uncle and cousins and grandparents, how terrified must he be when all he had was me?

"When you move, call here," I said, and read him Chris's number off the phone. It was an act of trust on my part, but I knew Chris wouldn't betray me, and I didn't have a lot of alternatives. "There's a housekeeper. Give her your name and tell her you're a friend of Chris and Amy's. Chris is my friend. He'll give me the message."

"I'm sorry, Brooke," he said. "I'm sorry it all turned out this way."

"I know," I said. "I'm sorry too."

14

Chris drove me back to the house. We didn't say much, since I had little to say, and he respected my silence. I liked Chris, liked pretty much all of the Freaks. I was just sorry I'd become one.

I unlocked the front door and was startled to see my mother standing there. "Where were you?" she cried. "Do you have any idea what time it is?"

I looked at my watch. "Five-twenty," I said. "Is that a problem?"

"I didn't know where you were," she said. "You didn't tell anybody you'd be late. I've been worried sick."

"Sorry," I said. "Next time I'll call."

"Don't use that tone with me," she said. "Tell me where you were."

I glanced at the living room. They were all there—Mike looking worried, Tim embarrassed, and Holly just a little bit pleased. My mother was clearly hysterical. The average American family, all right.

"I was at a club meeting," I said. "Then I went to my friend Chris's house, and then he drove me home. I'm sorry I didn't tell you. I didn't realize I had to account for every minute I spend away from this house."

"I didn't know you'd joined a club," Mike said. You could always count on Mike to go for the neutral territory. "Are you working on the school paper?"

The urge to lie was strong. I hadn't really lied about anything since I'd moved there, not the kind of lies that counted. Yes, I passed the test. No, I don't have any homework. Yes, the party will be chaperoned. I had three weeks' worth of lies I was entitled to. Yes, I've joined the school paper.

But the problem was I'd been lying about everything else in my life. Yes, I'm happy. Yes, things are fine. And I was tired of lying, almost as much as I was tired of being lied to.

"It's a support group," I said. "It meets once a week."

"What kind of support group?" my mother asked. "You don't need a support group."

"Kids, why don't you go to your rooms," Mike suggested. "Get a head start on your weekend homework."

"Dad, I don't want to do my homework," Holly said. "This is my house. I don't think it's fair I have to leave."

"My God," my mother said. "You drink."

"Who drinks?" I asked, hoping, for a moment, that she meant Holly.

"You do," she said. "That's it, isn't it? It was an Al-Anon meeting because you drink."

I stared at her. "I'm not going to have this conversation in front of an audience," I said. I thought about the blessed privacy of Chris's bedroom and wished I were back there.

"That's a good idea," Mike said. "Betty, why don't you and Amy talk in our room. The kids'll help me fix supper."

"Why can't we just watch TV?" Holly asked.

"Fine," Mike said. "Watch TV. Rot your bodies and your minds. See if I care."

"My stomach hurts," Tim said.

"You drink," my mother said as we walked up the stairs to her room. "I should have guessed. This is my worst nightmare come to life."

I didn't know what to tell her. I was afraid that admitting on occasion I had had a beer would push her over the deep end. So I kept quiet, and when we entered her bedroom, I closed the door behind us.

"How long have you been drinking?" she asked.

"I don't drink," I said. "Not the way you mean. It wasn't an Alateen meeting. It wasn't a meeting that had anything to do with drinking, or drugs, if you want to start worrying about that. It's just an informal group of kids who get together to talk about problems with their families."

"What problems?" she asked. "You don't have any problems."

I rolled my eyes. My mother stared at me, and then she laughed. "Sorry," she said. "I really am."

"I am too," I said. "I forgot that you worry about me

all the time. I'm not used to it. I had a lot of freedom with Dad. I'd let him know if I wasn't going to be home for supper, but that was the earliest I had to report in."

"I don't approve of that at all," she said. "Holly always has to let us know where she'll be after school."

"Holly's eleven," I said. "When I was eleven, I had to tell Dad that too."

"I'm sorry again," she said. "It's still like a dream to me, having you with me, and I think it's going to end, and I'll be back in that same endless nightmare. I know I worry too much. I know I'm overprotective. I know if my mother had done to me what I'm doing to you, I would have hated it. I know all of that, Amy. You're going to have to give me time to adjust."

"This isn't easy for any of us," I said.

"No, it isn't," she said. "Hal certainly saw to that."

I nodded. I wanted to get out of there, out of that room, but I didn't know where I could go to that I'd feel comfortable. The past three nights I'd dreamed that the canopy had fallen on my head and smothered me. Dreams like that don't endear a bedroom set to you.

"Is it a nice group?" my mother asked. "The kids with family problems."

"I like them," I said. "The problems vary. No one has a set just like mine."

"Can you tell me about them?" she asked.

"No," I said. "We have a confidentiality rule. What gets said at a meeting never leaves."

"I'm not sure I like that," she said. "Are you sure they're the kind of kids you want to hang around with?

Did your friends at your old school have family problems?"

"Some did, some didn't," I said. "I like these kids. I don't know if they're going to be my friends forever, but I don't really care. I've never had lifelong friends. I moved around too much."

"It breaks my heart what Hal did to you," my mother said. "I think about you growing up that way, lonely and sad, and I cry."

"I wasn't lonely," I said. "I wasn't sad. Don't cry."

She reached for me and touched my hand gently with hers. It still felt like an electric shock. "I'm going to make up for all of it," she said. "I'm going to give you the love you never had."

"I know," I said. "And I'm really very grateful. Thank you again, for everything you've done."

She stared at me. "You hate me, don't you," she said. "Hal poisoned you with his damned hatred for me, and nothing I've done has made a difference."

"No, of course not," I said. "I don't hate you."

She pulled her hand away from me and turned her face to the window. "I thought this would be so easy," she said. "I thought the years wouldn't matter, that inside you . . . you'd still be my Amy, my little girl. But you're not. That's what it comes down to, isn't it? You're not my little girl."

"No, I'm not," I said. "I'm sorry. I'd like to be." I thought she was going to start crying, and I wasn't sure I could deal with two sobbing parents in a single hour. "I look for Amy all the time," I said. "Inside me. I'm always asking myself if I remember something, if there are feelings inside me that were hers, that were mine I guess, eleven years ago."

"Have you found any?" my mother asked.

"I remember missing you," I said. "Dad says I cried every night after he told me you were dead. I'm not sure I remember crying, but I remember the loss, the fear, and the pain."

"But nothing from when we lived together," my mother said. "I keep hoping something will spark those memories. I was sure the kitten would." She faced me again and smiled. "I went to three animal shelters to find one that looked like Buttons," she said. "Not even that worked."

"Some of it'll come back to me," I said. "I'm sure of it. One day I'll see a picture or smell a flower and something will click. Maybe if we went to the house I used to live in."

"We can't," my mother said. "To be perfectly honest, we moved three times before you were four. And then the house that you and Mike and I lived in, the place Holly was born in, burned down about two years after we'd moved out. There's nothing left there that you could connect with."

"That figures," I said.

"It does, doesn't it," she said. "I have pictures from when you were a baby, but most of them are of you and Hal. I was the photographer in the family, and he loved having his picture taken with you. After the divorce, I don't know, I just stopped taking pictures. That wasn't a good time in my life. I didn't do things right for a while, not until I met Mike."

"It's okay," I said. "The feelings, the memories, they're all locked away inside me. They'll come out when they're ready."

"Will you love me then, do you think?" she asked. "I know you don't now. I see how you look at me. I hear the tone in your voice. I know you don't even know what to call me. Do you think that'll change? Do you think you'll love me again?"

"I want to more than you can imagine," I said. "Yesterday I looked at you and Holly and I thought that should be mine, that kind of love. It was stolen from me. I told him that, that he had no right to steal that love from me."

"Told who?" my mother asked.

"Dad," I said. "I told him."

"When?" she asked.

The volleyball game started again, only this time there were two teams, and they were both using my heart for a ball. "Today," I said. "This afternoon."

"Did you see him?" she asked. "My God, if he's in town, if he's made any effort to see you, I'll have him back in court, and this time I'll make sure he goes to prison."

"Stop it," I said. "I didn't see him. I called him from Chris's. That's what took me so long. I called to tell him how angry I was. I'd think you'd want that, I'd think you'd want him to know I hate him."

"I don't want you to even think about him," she said. "And I certainly don't want you to speak with him. You know you're not supposed to. The judge made that perfectly clear. These are the judge's rules, not mine, Amy. I can't believe you did that, you called him. Have you called him before? Have you been talking to him on a regular basis?"

"You want to know why I don't love you?" I said. "This is why."

She raised her hand to hit me and then with a horrified moan pulled it back. "I swore I would never do that again," she said.

"Yeah, I know," I said. "People do a lot of swearing around me."

"What do you want?" she asked. "Do you want to live with my parents? Do you want to spend next year in a boarding school? What is it you want?"

"I don't know," I said.

"Oh, come on now," she said. "You've been thinking night and day about what you want. You must have some idea."

"You know what I want? All right, I'll tell you," I said. "I want you to like me. I want that most of all. I want you to like who I am and what I've become, and then maybe you'll love me and then I can love you. That's what I want. I want you to love the me that I am and not some made-up five-year-old ideal of yours. I want you to love me the way other kids' mothers love them, the way you love Holly and Tim."

"But I do love you," she said.

"You're not listening," I said. "Love me, Brooke,

Amy, the name doesn't matter. But it has to be *me* you love."

Now she was crying. I had a real gift. Holly yesterday, Dad and my mother today. I remembered a time when I could have a conversation with people without them bursting into tears, but it was a lifetime ago. Literally.

"I'm sorry," I said, not because I was, but because that was what I had to say. "I didn't mean to make you cry."

"It's his fault," she said. "He's still poisoning you. You can't ever have anything more to do with him. Promise me that, Amy. Swear you won't ever call him again."

"No," I said. God, that word felt good. "I won't swear that."

"Then this is all for nothing," she said. "You'll never love me. You'll never belong. Is that what you want, to have a mother you don't love, because you insist on loving your father instead?"

"It's not a competition," I said. "I really think if you'd both give me the chance, I could love both of you. Dad was too afraid to. That's what it all came down to with him, just fear. I'd love you, I'd love Mike, I wouldn't possibly have any love left for him. And now you're saying the same thing. My God. I thought kids were supposed to have two parents to love. I thought hearts grew. That's what you told me when Holly born. You said hearts grow big enough for all the love they have to hold."

She stared at me. "You remembered," she said. "I told you that and you remembered."

"Yeah," I said. "I did, didn't I?"

"Oh, now I really am going to cry," she said, so of course she didn't. "You remembered that. I told Holly the same thing when Timmy was born. I told Timmy that the day we knew you were coming back to live with us. It's something I've always believed, the capacity the heart has for love. And you remembered. After eleven years you still remembered."

"I told you Amy was inside me," I said. "Dad didn't kill her. He just raised me a different way than you would have, and I'm a different person because of that."

My mother nodded. "He drives me crazy," she said. "I mean that, the very thought of him drives me crazy."

"I know and I'm sorry," I said. "But that's got to be your problem. I have enough of my own."

"I won't let you see him," she said. "The judge was absolutely right about that."

"I'm not asking to see him," I said. "He isn't asking to see me either. But I have to be able to speak to him. I have to be able to read his letters. I'm real sorry. I wish I didn't still love him. I'm so angry at him, it's burning me up inside. That's why I had to call him today, to tell him that, to let him know he's responsible for my pain. He can't avoid that responsibility."

"And what did he do?" she asked. "Did he try to charm his way out of it?"

"He cried," I said. "It wasn't charming."

"I'm not sure I ever loved him," my mother said. "He used to be so good-looking, and I was awfully young. Not much older than you are now. God." She paused for a moment. "If Mike knew how much cursing and blaspheming has been going on in here, he'd have a fit."

"I won't tell him if you don't," I said, and we smiled. I liked her smile, I realized. I hadn't seen enough of it to know that before.

"I don't know how to talk to you about him," she said. "For eleven years I've been consumed with hate. Before then too, really. I felt so trapped in that marriage. But I wanted you, I wanted you so much. And when Hal and I split up, I'd think no matter how much I hated him, you wouldn't have existed without him, and that made up for a lot."

I looked at my mother, really looked at her, and she returned my stare. It was the first time we'd ever honestly examined each other.

"When Hal took you, I had nothing left but the hate," she said. "Hate and terror. I pray you'll never know what that kind of hate and terror feels like."

I nodded. I'd had enough of a taste of those feelings the past few weeks to know what she was talking about.

"Sometimes when I look at you, I see Hal," my mother said. "His looks, his mannerisms, the way he raised you. And there's that eleven-year gap we can never close, and the hate and the terror floods back."

"Don't you like me at all?" I asked.

"I don't know yet," my mother said.

It hurt, but it was better than a lie. "I want that," I said. "I want you to like me. There's so much, I don't know if it's ever going to happen. Love. Trust. Dad did his best to see we'd never have that together, and I don't know if we ever will. But I used to be somebody people liked. Dad and Mona and my teachers and my friends and their parents. Lots of people used to like me. Mike likes me, I can tell. And that's so important to me, for you to like me, Brooke, Amy, whatever the hell my name is."

"Sometimes it's harder to like a person than to love her," my mother said. "I love Amy. I've loved her since the day she was born. But it's Brooke I have to like, and that's harder than I ever thought I'd admit."

"Do you think you ever will?" I asked.

My mother nodded. "Do you think you'll ever like me?" she asked.

I thought about her, about this woman I hardly knew, who had spent eleven years loving me on the strength of memory and faith. Eleven years where she loved her husband and raised her children and went to school and learned a trade and dealt with her parents and her brother and missing-children's bureaus. If we weren't related, if I'd just happened to hear her story, I would have thought her a remarkable woman.

"I like you already," I said. "It's just sometimes I'm so scared, I don't realize it."

"I forget you're scared," she said. "I'm sorry. That's important, and I should remember it."

"I should too," I said.

"It's all right," she said. "You've had a lot to remember since you got here. You don't have to add that to your list."

I felt funny then, sitting on my mother's bed, sharing such deeply personal confidences, saying things that most daughters never said to their mothers even if they needed to. I didn't know my mother, not really, and because I didn't know her, I didn't love her the way a daughter loves her mother. But that didn't mean I wouldn't love her someday, wouldn't like her, wouldn't trust in her love and her liking. It was going to take time, just the way everyone kept telling me. But we had time, and more than most daughters and mothers, we knew how precious that time was.

"I'm going to love loving you," I said.

My mother nodded. "I'm going to like liking you," she replied. "That's good. It means things are going to get better. Not everyone knows that about their future."

"We'd better go downstairs," I said. "They'll be worried."

We got up together and walked side by side down the stairs.

SUSAN BETH PFEFFER is the author of the highly praised *The Year Without Michael*—an ALA Best Book for Young Adults and a *Publishers Weekly* Best Book of the Year—and many other acclaimed young adult novels, including *Most Precious Blood*, *About David*, and *Family of Strangers*. She lives in Middletown, New York.